Terriers
IN THE
Jungle

Terriers
IN THE
Jungle

A NOVEL

GEORJA UMANO

atmosphere press

Published by Atmosphere Press

Library of Congress Control Number: 2021919959
ISBN: 978-1-63988-106-2

Cover design by Kevin Stone

Illustrations the work of Hilton Mghanga Mwakima and Moses Mugasia Misigo as well as other artists as listed in the back of the book.

Atmospherepress.com

Dedication

To the memory of **Dame Daphne Sheldrick**, *founder of the Sheldrick Wildlife Trust:*

Daphne, through love and kindness, has been responsible for rescuing and protecting hundreds of endangered African elephant orphans and their progeny.

*And also to Daphne's daughter, **Angela Sheldrick**:*

Angela continues to carry out and expand Daphne's mission of helping elephants and other wildlife throughout Kenya and engaging thousands of native and international supporters for African wildlife.

Chapter 1

ROMEO – A Home
Worth Waiting For

Last night I dreamt I sang with the elephants.

I'm a small dog, and I used to live in a gutter. It's taken me a long time, but I am starting to believe that my life is worthwhile. My name is Romeo, a terrier mix, probably a hodgepodge of Jack Russell and Rat terrier, with a touch of Chihuahua. And who knows where I got my big ears and red spots from? Along with my girlfriend Roxie, I'm the narrator of this story.

I had been surviving in trash and weeds on the side of the highway. My one friend was a little mouse who would come out of a hole in the ground and visit me. The only building nearby was a rundown bar called Booze Hounds with boisterous and rough-looking customers. The stale beer odor reeked out onto the street. A smashed-in wreck of a car lay curbside a few feet away. When it rained, I was grateful to crawl inside its stripped interior, although with my throbbing and injured back legs, I could barely move.

Most cars whizzed along with no notice of the shabby

corner where I survived. On the other side of the speedway, about a quarter mile away, I could see a large white edifice with columns and landscaping. From my perspective, it appeared to be a shining palace on a hill, close enough to see but impossible to reach—though I now believe it was probably a fancy Motel 6. But seeing it there, in its seeming grandeur, gave me an inkling that there *was* something nicer than what I was experiencing. It was a signpost for my dreams—a glimmer of life that *could be*.

I now share a home with Kate, my gorgeous and brilliant super-mom who welcomed me as her beloved pet, and with Roxie, my white-bearded terrier-princess, who was also adopted by Kate. When I met them, I became exuberant. It was the first time in my life I spun around for joy—something I have done gleefully hundreds of times since. Connecting with them was the most life-affirming, soul-healing event that could have happened to a wounded, homeless mutt.

There's no way I could have known at the time that Kate and Roxie needed me as much as I needed them. I later found out that Kate searched high and low for me. And when she saw a small photo of me, she knew right away that I was *the one*, and that our coming together was somehow meant to be.

Kate has a strong spiritual connection with animals, including a special love for her adopted baby elephants in Africa and us dogs. She had lost her wildlife photographer husband, Gerard, and believes she'll never find someone else like him again. On top of that, Kate and Roxie were grieving the death of their companion dog, Marcello.

So you can see, this was no casual adoption. The connections are deep: it is the fitting together of a much larger puzzle. We all love and respect each other for who we are. Fate brings us together, and our bonds will never be broken!

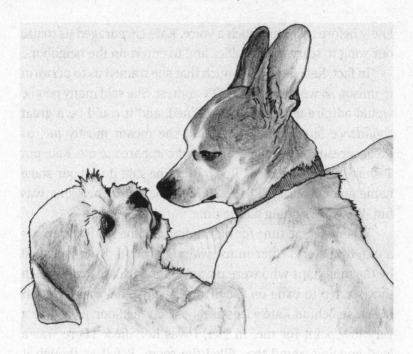

Kate and Roxie and I reside in a pretty townhouse near the Pacific Ocean in Santa Monica, California, where I've been learning many lessons to become a respectable pet. To me, *Nirvana* itself couldn't be better.

Roxie has been my shining star from day one. She has taken me under her wing, so to speak, and she and Kate have taught me everything from how to ride in a car, sleep in a dog bed, even run and play like a regular dog—and most of all, to enjoy life and to trust. I admire Roxie, who gets a kick out of abundant casual relationships with friends and acquaintances. Many people know her name, and she is friendly and available—unlike me, who is suspicious and awkward around new people.

I try to follow her every move, including her bark. When she barked her high-pitched yip one day, I let loose and followed up with my own unique sound, which was more like a tenor wolf howl, Kate said. It made a jolly tune, and so we would carry on and on as Kate laughed uproariously. I never knew before that I had such a voice. Kate encouraged us to use our song to scare away bullies and to entertain the neighbors.

In fact, Kate liked it so much that she trained us to perform in unison so we could enter a TV contest. She said many people would admire us and be entertained, and it could be a great *confidence builder* for us. I think she meant mostly *me*, as Roxie already seemed overconfident compared to me. Kate put T-shirts on us that read "Roc n Ro." She said it was our stage name and encouraged us to sing on cue. The rehearsing was fun. We were singing all the time.

When it came time for our audition at the studio, that was a different story. After much waiting around, I was spooked by the musicians who were placed behind us, especially when they started to bang on the drums. I got so nervous I ran off the stage behind Kate's legs and peed on the floor. That was a very low point for me. In fact, I was horrified. There was a loud gonging sound that filled the room. It felt as though it was reverberating all the times in my life when I didn't make the cut.

Like in the shelter, where I was kept for a while and was not adopted. I was taken down that ominous hallway from which dogs don't return. It was only by a moment of grace I was saved when that young woman, Charlene, ran down the hall huffing and puffing. She stopped the man who was carrying me at the very last second before we entered the euthanasia room. I'm so grateful to Charlene and the Dexter Foundation who rescued me before I breathed my last breath. Ricarda, the founder of the rescue group, took me to a doctor and saved me yet again—when the doctor wanted to amputate my left leg. She talked him into inserting a steel plate instead. And that was followed by months and months of healing in cages in foster homes before I finally met my own loving family.

I worried whether the loves of my life, Kate and Roxie,

would still want me and hold me dear after the TV debacle. I held my breath. I became extra sensitive to moods and on the lookout for negative feelings. Luckily for me, nothing changed. Even though we were all disappointed that we didn't win the free trip to New York, no one ever chastised me or treated me differently. Kate said we would just have to "give it more time" until I felt more secure. It was never mentioned again after that.

***

At Christmastime, Kate decided we should go visit her mother, Grandma, who is staying in a town in Oregon. Kate packed our things and she loaded up the car. Having never been on a trip before, I wasn't sure what to expect. I didn't understand what Christmastime was about. Kate said, "It's the time of year when we like to visit friends and family. There may be festivities while we're there, like people singing Christmas songs, and maybe there will be a pretty Christmas tree." I felt excited.

Then we drove, and drove, and drove. All the way up the long California coast. We got out of the car to look at the sea otters along the way. So cool! They're like little dogs who live in the water. Kate took lots of pictures. At night we stopped in motels on the way. We even stopped in a fancy Motel 6! (That's when my *mind* was really spinning!) During the days on the road, I looked out the car window and saw lots of empty streets. I was reminded of my vagabond roots. I felt safe and secure in the car with my very own mom and my girlfriend. I was so relieved that street living was behind me.

The more we drove, the chillier it became. Mom put both our sweaters and our jackets on us when we went outside, but we still couldn't get warm enough. When we had to pee, we did our business but ran back in the car.

We finally got to Oregon, and in Grandma's town, there was snow on the ground. I had never seen that before. But after Roxie and I got used to it, we loved playing and sliding in it. We got more used to the cold and began jumping around in the snow. We chased each other around in the drifts. Kate joined in for some snowball throwing. Snow is exciting! She had trouble getting us to come back inside! But, once we were back someplace warm, we didn't want to go outside again for a long time.

Grandma lives in an apartment building where lots of old people live. She didn't want us to get up on her furniture, but she was friendly to us. Roxie and I felt pleased to meet new people who are part of our family. Kate got worried about us making noise and bothering people. The old people who live in the building do not like noise. Singing was definitely not allowed. Outside it was still freezing cold. Not too much for dogs like us to do.

Kate doesn't like to be cold either. She took us out in the backyard of the retirement building and let us run off leash in the deep snow. It was fun for a while—until it started to sleet. We were getting so cold and wet by then that we pounced right back toward the door. Then suddenly, we found something large in the snow. At first, we didn't know what it was, but it started to move and make a noise. It was an old man. He had snow all over him and not too many clothes. Roxie and I barked and jumped up and down. Kate yelled from inside the door, "Come in, it's cold!"

Roxie and I looked at each other. We knew we had to help Kate find the old man. So instead of running toward her as we would usually do, we stayed with the man, and we kept jumping and barking. She came over to see what was going on. "What is it, guys?" She saw the man. "Oh, no! Great work! Very good doggies! Thank you for letting me know. Come on, we'll go get help." She comforted the man, "Don't worry, sir,

8

help is on the way." We could barely see with the sleet on our eyes, but we trudged our way back to the door. There was an alarm going off. We raced up the steps and over to the front desk.

Kate told the receptionist, "A man outside is stuck in the snow. It's very cold. Please send somebody right away!" There was a lot of commotion as the lady called people to help. We had to go back outside to show them where the man was. The sleet was now a blizzard and it was coming down so hard that we could barely see at all. We were worried that we might get stuck out there and freeze—or suppose we couldn't find our way back? Kate said to the responders, "The dogs found him. I think they'll be able to lead us back."

So Roxie and I led the way, though it was even harder to get through the blizzard than we thought. We stayed as close to each other as possible, each one of us helping to guide the other. We were a real team. But it seemed like it was taking forever to get back to the place where we found the man. Finally, we saw him. He was almost completely covered in snow.

"Quick, call an ambulance!" someone shouted. That was a relief. Now that the rescue folks were on the way, we could go inside. We and Mom pushed ourselves back through the blizzard towards the door as best we could. Our paws were freezing!

We climbed back upstairs panting towards Grandma's warm apartment. All those people on the first floor looked at us like we were brave and courageous, which we *were*. I thought we might expect praise from Grandma, too. Grandma was sitting on the couch with a funny look on her face. In a scolding voice, she said to Kate, "There you are! I wondered where you went. You've always liked spending your time playing with animals. I guess you haven't changed." Uh oh. From the tone of her voice, it sounded like a put-down.

Kate looked at us, and we looked at Kate. We could tell that there was pain in her heart. Roxie and I kissed her hand. She smiled at Grandma and nodded. There was a long pause, then Mom offered to get Grandma some tea. We both sat down on the rug, quiet as mice. Later, Grandma heard about our brave rescue from the office people. We heard her tell her friends about it, as though she was *proud* of us after all.

There was a large group of her friends all gathered downstairs by a Christmas tree singing carols. She invited us to come downstairs with her. It was exciting to me, as it was my first Christmas celebration ever. As we sat patiently nearby while she sang, she patted our heads. We got lots of smiles from her friends. People came up to us and told us we were good dogs—and heroes! At the end of "Jingle Bells," Roxie and I looked at each other. We saw Kate smiling. Roxie started in with her little barks and I joined in. We gave them a thrill hearing our rousing song. Some of them held their ears like they hurt, and others laughed. At the end, some of them clapped, and then they all joined in. So finally, we enjoyed our time in the spotlight!

A few days later, it was time to get back on the road.

Driving home in the car, Kate explained that some people do not understand animals or how other people can love them so much. When she was a little girl, her uncle let her pick out a dog in the shelter for Christmas. Kate said she and her mom had just moved to a new neighborhood. Her dad was in the Army and had to go out of town to work. She didn't have any friends.

When we got to the motel that evening, Mom continued her childhood story. Her dog, Bernie, became her best friend and she loved him so much. Their landlord didn't like dogs and said they would have to move. Kate was so upset that she tried to run away with Bernie. It caused a lot of problems for her mom, even after they caught up with her. The police took

Bernie away. Grandma never let her have any pets after that. Kate got very sad as she remembered Bernie and even got tears. Roxie and I cuddled with her and licked her face.

We were relieved when we got back home. No more wearing sweaters or jackets all the time. A little rain no longer bothered us. We learned a lot about life. And about people, too. Although Kate has a heart of gold for animals, her mother doesn't feel the same. Roxie and I share lots of love with our mom. I bet there are a lot of dogs—even what they call "purebreds"—who never get to experience so much love and learn all the things we do. I was starting to feel more and more like I belonged and was needed—like an important part of this little family.

***

A few weeks ago, Kate's father, Horace, came to visit. He and Grandma have been separated for a long time and he was feeling lonesome. He and Kate decided the best thing would be if he stayed with us for a while. He could enjoy our company and help Kate take care of us at the same time. He's a mellow guy, very soft-spoken and he seems to like me and Roxie, and we like him, too.

Now, however, Kate is planning a big trip to Africa. She'll write articles about conservation and explore ways to help elephants! We dream about seeing the elephants that Mommie talks about. She's going to take Grandpa with her. Roxie is an optimist. She thinks Mom will take *us* with her, too.

A few days later, Kate announces that she's decided we will *all* relocate to Kenya to live. She wants to be of value in elephants' lives like she is in mine and Roxie's. I don't relish the idea of leaving our comfortable castle by the sea, but I am beguiled because I think elephants must be something extraordinary. After all, Kate loves them so much that she's willing to drag us halfway around the world. I feel pretty sure that I will love them, too.

Kate had met elephants a few times before when she visited Africa. She went on excursions with her photographer husband, Gerard. It was her favorite thing to do. I heard her tell her friend, Golda, all about it on the phone "The last trip Gerard made to Africa, I wasn't able to go. My mom was ill and I wanted to help her. Gerard was like a young David Attenborough, eager to learn more about all species, every chance he got. He was riding in a small plane in the Congo when it crashed..." She couldn't tell the story without breaking down in tears.

That happened two or three years ago. Now she feels ready to go back to Africa, and with Horace coming too, we will *all* be able to go and stay longer. She says the elephants are in trouble from people poaching them and others not protecting them, and she feels in her heart that *they want her* to come back. She tells Roxie and me how much she loves Africa but that it can also be dangerous. So it is very important for Roxie and me to listen to her very well and do just what she says. Roxie and I look at each other in wonderment.

Neither Roxie nor I have seen any elephants in person, and I am still confused about them. Kate says they are gigantic, but in her pictures of them, and even on TV programs, they look small. Are elephants like pets and family members? I can't figure it out. She admires them so much, she has pictures and statues of them all over the house. Suppose she likes elephants more than she likes us? That's the scariest question—what will happen to us if she wants to stay in Africa for good? Maybe she would not have time for us in that case?

She only left town without us one time before, and I was almost falling apart, even though a nice dog sitter named Carl took care of us while she was gone. At the thought of being separated from her, I brood and whine. Kate tells me, "Let's all act more elephant! Elephants are brave and kind. The families stick together and help one another." I want to make her proud. I wish I *were* an elephant. But I'm only a dog, and, as much as I may want to be something else, I can't be.

Kate brings our cookies in her pocket when we go out for walks. She bribes us to "sit" and "be quiet" all along the way. Kate says she's teaching us to go on a long airplane ride. She says that she may need our help to hear and be aware of some things. That's why we're learning to pay more attention. We'll be her service dogs. I feel glad we're able to help her. It makes me feel more elephant. I wonder if she knows that I would do anything in the world to help her. She's my one and only mom, and I would protect her with everything I've got.

But somehow, deep down inside, I can't believe she will *really* bring us along. Here comes Carl for a chat, and I'm thinking it must be to pick up our house keys. When she leaves, I'll have to go through so much pain and drama all over again. *It's too much to bear.* What can I do? I bear it.

Kate realizes I am acting moody and she tells us again, emphatically, that we're *all* going to Africa! I'm still uneasy. It's like when she leaves the house, she tries to make me feel better and says, "I'll be back real soon." But sometimes it's *hours* before I see her again! No matter what Kate says or how many treats she gives me, I'm still worried she's going to leave without me.

I want to cry out, but I can't speak English. *Don't go!* It gets worse and worse because she won't stop talking about it. Kate realizes how I feel. She says, "Don't worry, my sweet boy. We are *all* going on a great adventure together. You will meet an elephant, I'm sure of that."

That's great, Mom. Later my nerves kick in again. We didn't go there before—so why would we go now? Every day when she's excited and making plans for the trip, I want to cry, "Don't leave me, Mommie! Please!"

***

The day of departure comes. Kate is cheerful. "Come on darlings, let's make sure we are all packed up and ready to go. We may find a beautiful place to live in Africa and *never even come back!*"

Roxie smiles, "Okay Mom! We're ready to go."

Meanwhile, I'm thinking, "'*Never come back*?' What does that mean? Where in the world would we go where we *never wanted to come back home?* Home is paradise. Home is where it's at. How can she be so casual about leaving it all behind?"

Roxie muses, "It must be some place really nice, Romie. Sometimes you just have to take a chance or you will never learn anything. Kate and Horace will be there. They'll take care of us. Don't get yourself in a pickle."

Kate calls us, "Come on, let's go to the park and run around. We need to get tired out so we can sleep on the plane. Who wants to go to the park?"

"*Okay, Mom. That's always fun.*" I trudge along but still with a long face. We jump in the back seat of her car on our fake leopard dog beds, as usual. Clover Park is about a mile away from home. We get out and tear across the lawn, pulling on Kate and our leashes. She laughs.

Soon, we are chasing each other around the field. It's nearly empty at midday, so she lets us run off-leash. We run and we roll down the hill. I'm not very good at rolling, but I follow Roxie's lead, and soon I am forgetting all my problems and trying to catch her. We rest a minute, then get up and run some more. A gorgeous Southern California day.

Kate loves to go on walks, and she likes to play with us and meet other dogs. She even rolled down the hill with us that day. Sometimes I wonder if she isn't part dog herself. Horace doesn't walk as much, and he likes to sit at a desk. Maybe it's because he's old.

We get ourselves nice and tired, then we go home and Kate gives us a warm bath. In the beginning, baths freaked me out. When she would put me into the tub, I would jump right out. But I've come to enjoy the feeling of warm water on my fur, getting my teeth brushed, too. And I love shaking it off and getting towel-dried and hugged by you-know-who.

It's nighttime. They're putting all the suitcases in a taxi, and we're going to the airport.

The airport is noisy, but we are quiet. We get on the plane, and the space is so small where we have to stay. We're quiet. We get treats. Best of all, it looks like *we're all* going to Africa! Kate says we are first going to New York to see some friends. *I'm not getting left behind!* I kiss her hand. Now I'll be more elephant! Everything gets dark, and I fall asleep. When I wake up, we're in New York. Is *Africa* another word for *New York*?

After getting off the plane, they collect all the suitcases and we jump into a taxi. I'm not left behind. *They love me! They really, really love me!* We finally get to our New York room. Mom takes us for a walk. We walk and walk, and we see a tree, but when we get near it, it has a fence around it. Any grass we feel like sniffing has metal bars in front of it. We pass a little park but we can't get in. What the heck? Mom sees we're reluctant to walk. She says we're heading to a different area now, and we may be pleasantly surprised. She must know something we don't know. We come to what looks like a big park. As before, we see it has a fence around it. Wait a minute. *Hey! There's a big entranceway!* It's okay to go in! We get excited!

Central Park! Lots of grass and trees and new smells all around us! This must be Africa! I keep a lookout for elephants and lions to pop out from behind the bushes. We don't see any yet, but we love the spring flowers and shrubs. There's a lake. We go to an outdoor restaurant and meet Kate and Horace's friends. We aren't in New York more than two or three days when Mom packs up our things and we go back to the airport. I think we're going home to California.

That airport is another hurdle. It is bad enough that we have to mind our manners and keep our mouths shut, but when I hear Kate stutter and raise her voice, I perk up my ears. A guy wearing a badge tells her they can't have dogs on the plane. She says she sent in papers, but he says they don't have those papers. *Grr.* I want to bite the guy who says dogs can't go on the plane. But I wouldn't dare. I'm a good dog, quiet and still, like she taught me to be. Kate acts like *she* is either going to bite or have a meltdown.

These louts want to separate us from the humans who love us? *I don't think so!* I *would* start howling, but I remember her training to keep my mouth shut—and that's what I do. What happens if they don't let dogs go? Would we have to stay at the airport? I don't think Mom would leave without us. *Bad thoughts.* Kate is persistent. Nothing is going to stop her from getting to Africa and seeing those elephants. And she's *not* leaving us behind!

Finally, a lady supervisor comes over. She says it's okay to bring us on the plane. *Whew!* It's good to have a mother who fights for us. Roxie and I sigh and gaze at each other. We wait around the airport for a while longer. Then we get on another airplane. I think, "So this is what she does when she leaves us at home?" I'm surprised because the airplane part isn't much fun.

Now Roxie is going to tell you what happens next.

Chapter 2

ROXIE – Monkeying Around

Yes, it's me, Roxie!

Before we know it, we're leaving New York and on another plane. This time it's bright and sunny outside. As the plane goes up, I think about birds. I was always curious about how they flew and lived up high in the tree. We're still lifting up. Stomach, here we go again. For some reason I start thinking about the other time in my life when I was up high—hanging in a bird's nest. I chuckle a little to myself. I daydream about that day so long ago when I was a street dog with my brother Rex. He had been sick as a puppy and I always tried to cheer him up. I like to take care of those I love and make sure they're okay. But sometimes, things get out of control.

Rex and I slept in an abandoned yard. To have fun, every day we looked for new challenges. I was trying to open Rex's eyes to all the critters around us, kind of like Kate does.

One lazy summer day was the last time I saw his puppy face. I lured him into a dangerous adventure. "Look, Rex!" I said, "We could climb up that tree!" Rex smiled at me, his eyes twinkling. There were no workmen in sight as we rushed to the back of the cable truck and pawed up a slippery ramp at the back. We hopped across the truck bed to the wide-step ladder that was propped up against a tree. I carefully pulled myself up, to the very top rung and took a glimpse at what lay below on the ground. Never been so high before. It made me feel woozy.

"Don't look down, Rex!" I warned him. I felt a tree branch by my nose and jumped onto it.

He was a few steps below. He glared up at me, "What do you think we are, cats?"

"Come on—you can do it!"

Rex hesitated.

Meanwhile, two workmen in uniforms returned to the truck. The chubby, bearded one spotted Rex. He called out to the tall one, "Tom, look at the puppy up on the ladder!"

Tom rushed over to the ladder. He said, "Don't worry, little fellow. We'll get you down," as he climbed up. I watched from above, hidden among leaves. Tom grabbed Rex gently and set him down on the back of the truck bed. Rex looked *right up toward me* in the tree and *barked. Rex, you're not too savvy.* He kept barking until the men looked up in my direction. They still couldn't see me though. *Heh heh!*

"He's probably barking at a squirrel. Are you out hunting, little buddy?" Tom chuckled.

"Hey, he doesn't have a collar," said the bearded one. "Are you a stray? Maybe we need to take you to the shelter."

What? Alarms went off in my head. I didn't want Rex to be taken anywhere. *Oh, no!* I had to rescue Rex. *How was I supposed to get back down the tree?* I tentatively inched down the trunk. With my nails, I scraped the sides of the tree to find a lower branch, and I slipped into freefall. I barely glommed onto a lower branch—my paw landing halfway inside a bird's nest. I was hanging and panting. Baby birds opened their tiny beaks and squeaked, "Cheep-cheep-cheep." *They thought I was going to feed them! Heh Heh!*

A huge mother crow appeared and jabbed at my ear. *Grr-ow!* I growled back at the crow. The guys in the truck looked up.

"There's a dog in the tree!" the bearded one said.

Tom climbed up the ladder and reached for me with his long arm. I got a whiff of his tuna fish breath. My stomach grumbled. "Aw, look at this—they're twins!" he shouted. I backed away as far as I could, and I smashed against the tree trunk. He grabbed at me with his gigantic hand. I backed off some more—into *thin air.* I was falling through space!

Whap! I landed on the beard of the bearded one. "Ouch!" he screamed as my nails pulled at the wiry hairs on his face. I could see Rex standing beside a canvas that was bunched up on the bed of the truck. Praying for a soft landing, I twisted with all my might and dived off the guy's beard. I crashed onto the canvas.

"Whoops! My breath felt stuck in my stomach for a long moment. The air finally came back out. The two dudes stared at me wide-eyed, their mouths gaping. Rex and I took off down the ramp. We slid to the side and slipped straight down only to plop into a deep, muddy puddle. My whole head landed in the mud. *Yuck!* Rex got drenched, too. My paw slipped again as I struggled my way out of the muddy mess. We heard the workmen guffawing like it was the funniest thing they'd ever seen. Rex and I ran off as fast as we could. Soon we were racing like the wind.

We darted around the corner and the next one and the next. It looked like we'd lost them. *Uh oh!* Just as we relaxed our gait, we spotted the truck behind the tree, still parked in the same spot. We sneaked back near our yard and hid behind a bush. The truck finally pulled out. Rex blurted, "What on earth do you think we are, squirrels? Or maybe you thought we could fly like a bird?"

"If *they* can do it—I don't know why *not*," I joked. *"Heh*

heh!" Rex and I snickered and did a high-pitched bark in our special way. We chuckled and chortled. We walked to our yard. The people had moved out a while ago. But we still thought it was ours.

"Oh, Roxie, you look so funny!" I had mud on my eyebrows, my whiskers, my ears, and all over my body.

"At least we got away. I'll always keep you safe, little brother." He jumped playfully on my back and we rolled around in the untamed lawn among scattered fast-food containers and soda cans.

Our bowls were empty as usual, and the front door was closed. Recently, there had been squatters in the house, and sometimes they threw us leftovers. At dusk we could catch up with the neighborhood garbage strays, a small gang of cats and dogs who know how to pry open waste bins. I yawned. My eyelids snapped shut and I fell quickly asleep.

Twilight time. Sirens hurt my ears. Men in uniform were walking up the porch steps and coming inside the house. I popped up and scrambled around the yard. "Rex?" I barked and yipped, but he didn't answer. I scanned the yard. *Maybe he was in the house?*

I sneaked up onto the porch and slithered past the small crowd gathered near the door. A stocky man whose boot brushed against me nearly kicked me in the side. Too smart to let out a bark, I held my breath. Then I ran through his legs toward the front door. Suddenly I was being grabbed by the scruff of my neck. "Look who we have here!" he smirked. I growled as ferociously as I could, I tried to bare my teeth to scare him, but with my crooked overbite, it doesn't really work, so I nipped at his hand and tried to scratch at him. He held me away from his body in mock fear. "Ah! A scrappy little coyote!" The guy carried me back toward the street like I was a trophy. He dropped me inside an empty car and slammed me in. I heard the door lock. My heart was pounding.

Soon, a different large man opened the door and took me back out. Even though my adrenaline was pumping, for a moment it made me chuckle that all these big guys could barely capture a little girl like me. *Wait till they see a princess warrior escape! Heh heh!* I perused his long legs as I planned my leap to freedom.

He whisked me into a cage and left me inside a dark truck. I yelped and barked like crazy and hoped Rex would hear me. I'd escaped from tight spots before. I reminded myself to slow down and pace myself. He started up the truck. I smelled fumes. When it stopped, it jolted me back and forth so I could hardly catch my breath. We rode like that for a while, then on the last jolting stop, I heard muffled sounds of dogs—lots of dogs barking and howling. I was shuffled into a big pen with befuddled and scared dogs. I stood frozen as this new reality hit me. *Why is this happening?*

My eyes popped wide open. *The workmen!* They wanted to take us to a shelter! If I had let Rex take his nap instead of egging him to climb the ladder, we wouldn't be in this mess right now! An unusually loud and mournful yelp escaped from my lungs as karma came crashing down on me.

A brown-and-white spaniel came close and sat next to me, saying, "It's not so bad. A shelter is a place for dogs with no home. This is a no-kill shelter. That means, although the shelter people don't know you, they will protect you until you get a new home."

I looked in her cloudy eyes and replied, "I don't want a new home. I want my brother and our yard! Okay, sometimes we were almost hit by cars or didn't get enough to eat, but we had each other. It was a fun life." I teared up.

She said, "Being here means you won't be wandering the streets or starving to death if no one wants you anymore. Pretty soon, someone nice may come along and give you a new home." The spaniel's friend, who had been listening to our conversation, chimed in.

"I'm Fifi. I've been left here twice, and I want to give you a word of advice. If you get adopted, you must be nice. Don't have a bad attitude. Otherwise, they can bring you back here to the shelter!"

***

The plane jolts suddenly, shaking my eyes open and jogging me back to present reality. Whoops, I almost fly off my seat. I look up at Kate. I like to help her take care of things but this plane ride is making me feel totally out of control, just as I did when I was separated from Rex. She looks down at me and gives me a big hug and holds me on her lap. I'm so lucky to have my mom.

This is a very long ride. It's hard to sleep *all* the time. I'm excited and my mind is racing. It feels like another big change in my life is about to happen.

When we finally arrive at the next airport, Kate says we're in Amsterdam. She knows we have to *go* as we've been holding it in for hours. She asks lots of different people at the airport for a place where a dog can pee, but they look at her strangely as if she has asked them how to get to the moon. She asks someone else, "Do they have a place for dogs to go wee wee?" No answer.

"Dogs, pee pee? You know, bathroom?"

"Vat? No understand, Madame."

"I read you have a special place for dogs to go?"

"Don't know vat you mean, Madame," was the reply.

They have silly sounding accents. I could enjoy it more if I didn't have to *go* so badly. In desperation, we search for a door to get outside. Kate keeps telling us, "Hold on, guys! We'll find a spot for you to pee!" We skip across the room on the bottom floor of the airport and get out through a small opening.

22

Horace follows us and goes through the door. I feel a cold draft on my nose and cool drizzles landing on my coat. Kate walks us up a path, and what do you know? There is a park with a pond. New smells, new grass. Places to pee! Yay! It feels good to be outdoors.

Kate walks and jogs us around that pond a few times. Horace waits on the bench. He wants to eat. A tall hotel with a restaurant is perched on the side of the little park, and we all go in. No customers are around, so they say we can sit at a table in the back. We gobble up a few bites of cornbread and toast. Mom says we can't eat much because we have some more traveling to do. *What the heck!* So, this isn't Africa, either. She shivers. "Africa will be warmer," she says.

Before we know it, we're on yet another plane. Mom gives me some more medicine so the planes do not bother my stomach. As long as she is holding me and I can look out the window, I'm pretty good. More hours for us to be still and quiet. Dozing is fine, but you can only doze for so long. *So, this long ride is what Kate trained us for.* Romeo falls fast asleep. I start to daydream some more about my early life.

From the first minute Kate met me, she was warm and affectionate. That was when Gerard was still alive. He liked me a lot, too. And there was Marcello, the handsome and clever Jack Russell terrier who was her first dog. He came with them to the shelter to get me. I was both excited and nervous to leave with them that day. As we walked outside, I looked behind at the shelter. I thought I had heard Rex's voice in there and hoped against hope we could be reunited somehow. I promised myself, right there and then, that we *would* be reunited. We *had* to be. I couldn't imagine my life without him. So, I said a kind of prayer deep in my heart. One day I will find him. Let it be so.

Marcello didn't talk to me much but when he did, he would tell me to "calm down" and "go with the flow." I couldn't believe it when we got to our beach townhouse and they actually wanted me to stay *inside*. Cozy and comfortable, with dog beds on every floor—it was the lap of luxury. As I looked around at my new home, I noticed a statue of a dog that looked just like Marcello. I remember thinking that they must really like dogs if they even get a *statue* of a dog that looks like their *real* dog. But I couldn't allow myself to enjoy anything too much as long as I was worried about Rex.

Kate tried to name me Sophia. I would get up and walk out of the room so she knew I wasn't Sophia. She tried out more names. Finally, she stumbled upon Roxie. I looked at her and that's how she somehow knew that was my name. Out of all the millions of dog names, she was able to find mine! Then she said she would contact the shelter and find out more about my background. I started thinking that maybe she was psychic. I got my hopes up pretty high. It turned out she was able to find out I had a brother named Rex, but she also learned that he had already been adopted. It hit me hard. I may not ever see him again. I put my head down and sulked. I felt so alone. I promised myself again, "I will find Rex someday." Now Kate and Gerard and Marcello were all I had. Even though I thought they were nice, I did not appreciate all they were giving me.

When I was still pretty new to the family, Kate had to go out of town for two days. Gerard would take care of me, she said. But Gerard had a long business meeting one day, so she had arranged for someone else to come take us for a walk.

The next morning, she fed us, took us for our walk, and left. Then Gerard left. Later, a strange man showed up at our house. Marcello and I heard heavy footprints on the walkway. We approached the door like alert guard dogs. The guy must have had a key because he opened our front door. A shudder went down my spine. The man reached down with his big hands.

Oh! No! No! No! Not this again! No way am I going back

to the animal shelter! I leaped through his arms. I slipped out the opening in the door and took off running as fast as I could. I left that guy in the dust! Just like the days with Rex, I ran and ran—but I didn't know where I was going.

The guy tried to catch me, but he couldn't keep up. Pretty soon, other people were chasing me, too, and they were all yelling at me. I ran across streets and between cars. I remembered darting around trucks in my old life, and I still had those skills. *Heh heh!* It flashed through my mind that *I was completely free.* I could run away! I savored the wind on my face and the feeling of freedom. I remembered the times Rex and I ran fast, escaping from trucks and sometimes even gunshots. Afterwards, we hooted and hollered when we escaped, then rolled around with high energy in the grass.

After the momentary thrill, it didn't feel so exciting now that I was alone. Rex and I knew we would always be together and we could go back to the yard, our home base. It felt good to have a home base. I thought about Kate and Gerard who really liked me and wanted to give me a home. And my cushy dog bed. And the idea that I could always stay *inside*! I heard cars honking. A van slammed on the brakes and screeched loudly, almost hitting me—but I got away. Neighborhood people on foot caught a glimpse of me and came running.

I outsmarted every one of them and escaped from them all. Then, when no one was looking, I ran back to the house. I didn't think twice. My instincts led me directly back to my new home. When we were sniffing grass in the backyard the day before, I had noticed a tiny opening under our gate. Now I was plotting how that gap would come in handy. I'd lie on the ground and slither under it. Just like I used to squeeze through the planks in the fence at my old yard. I hoped I wouldn't get stuck like I once did over there. Rex had to push me through from the rear! But luck was with me. I was still skinny enough to squeeze through and make it into the backyard! *Hooray!*

I skipped up the steps. The sliding bedroom door was open slightly, and I pushed through the opening with all my might. I was inside. I jumped into my bed. My safe, wonderful bed.

The place was empty. I guessed that guy was still dragging Marcello around with him trying to find me. *Heh heh!* I took a long, slow drink of water, then went down by the front door and relaxed—waiting patiently for it to open. I heard footsteps. The door opened, and there they were. Marcello was his usual cool self. The man was sweating and out of breath. If he dared try to catch me again, I was prepared to hightail it out the back door.

When the guy saw me sitting there, he appeared so overwhelmed. It looked like he might keel over. The man quietly unleashed Marcello and slipped away! I gave myself a laugh over that one. *I bet he won't try that again!* I thought smugly. I started to feel like my old self.

Gerard came home and acted friendly, like nothing had changed. I pondered, *What about Kate?* The dog sitter would probably tell her about my disobedient adventure. She hadn't gotten mad at me so far, but I wondered if this prank would change anything.

That spaniel's fateful words were still ringing in my head. I did not want to be returned to the shelter. Fortunately, nobody got mad. Kate and Gerard thought it may have been a scary experience for me, being confronted by a stranger. After all, I was new. I was uncertain about my life. To them, I'd shown that I have guts. It was finally getting through to them—they had adopted a *warrior princess! Heh heh!*

The doorbell rang. I flew downstairs barking—to give proper warning. Kate followed and opened the door. No one was there. On the ground we saw a small box—which I viciously attacked. I jumped on it and growled and dug into it. I thoroughly demolished it and everything in it. I felt like the leader of a bomb squad, here to save the world from certain annihilation. Now Kate could get an eyewitness view of my bravery. I was so engaged with my mission that I didn't pay attention when she said, "It's okay, Roxie, it's just a little present from Grandma—*for you!*"

Her words finally penetrated. *What?*

Inside the battered box was a cute stuffed doggie doll—like the one that looks like Marcello, except this one looked just like me! Only problem was, I'd torn its head off! I slinked back into the house, humiliated. From the very next day, I started to feel more comfortable in my new home. It was easy to love Kate and Gerard.

I smile to myself on the plane. I'm finally able to doze off.

***

When I open my eyes, I see the plane has landed and people are starting to collect their things. We have to make sure we have all our stuff, and Kate has to squish our dog beds back into her huge backpack. We finally get off the plane. The air is warm and humid. I think people are speaking English, but it's a completely different sound. I can't pick up on any words. We can't even tell if they're speaking with accents. People look at me and Romeo and their eyes pop wide. They want to know all about us. Getting lots of attention—that part is fun.

But it looks like Kate is getting hassled about us again at the airport. She's struggling to work something out with people wearing badges. She has to pay them some extra money for "transporting livestock." She tells Horace that it's ridiculous, but better to pay, and just leave the airport.

A friendly man named Jackson picks us up in his car and drives. We head for the place where we'll be staying. There are several little cottages spread out on a grassy landscape. It's a little bit like Central Park but not as big. It has lots of shrubs and trees and the air smells really fresh. Kate and Horace say,

"Welcome to Africa!" and they hug. They hug us dogs and welcome us too. I think about Gerard and how it would have been great to share this adventure with him, too. I bet Kate is thinking the same thing. We discover that, yes, this is Africa, but it's Tanzania, another stopover before we get to Kenya, a *different* African country. And *that's* where we're going to live.

We stay a few days, and we walk around the yard and around the town. A few people ask Kate about us, as though they haven't seen many dogs before. They sure are hard to understand when they talk. Kate is friendly to them but keeps us safe on a short leash.

Jackson drives us around the area. We go to an outdoor restaurant to eat and celebrate that we've finally made it to Africa. It's Kate's birthday. We go to a store and Horace buys her a special bracelet. Mommie shows it to us. It's got a pretty blue stone called *tanzanite* that comes from Mount Kilimanjaro nearby. Then she puts it on her wrist.

We return to our little bungalow, and we all sleep hard. The next day, we visit a veterinarian who checks all our vaccinations and gives us some new ones for Africa. We were already checked by two different vets at home. This part is intimidating for me, and especially for Romeo. But Mommie is close by, so we are both brave and quiet.

After that ordeal, Jackson drives us outside the town for a hike around a big lake. Romie and I roll in the grasses and sniff around the trees. We sit with Kate and Horace and look out over the water. The skies are filled with gigantic white birds called giant egrets. The air smells sweet. The next couple of days we mostly rest in the park around our bungalow. We enjoy taking a breather. Next comes a long car ride in Jackson's van toward our new home. We're all feeling relaxed. No more planes—but lots of driving. We pass through a border.

At the checkpoint, a man comes out and grills Kate with

many questions. "Where are you from? Where are you going? Why do you have the dogs? Do they have papers? Can I see the papers?" And on and on. Mostly, he wants to know about us dogs. I can't understand him very well. Kate shows him papers, and he makes us wait around a long time. Romie and I feel nervous. We have to stay quiet. We can't figure out what's so unusual about two small dogs. At home, there are several of our type on every block. Finally, we get the go-ahead to keep driving. We're all relieved.

***

We've finally arrived in Kenya, which is where we are planning to stay. By the early evening, we smell beach air and we stop to rest for the night. It's a town called Diani Beach. Jackson finds us a little house with a yard to stay in.

Oh my goodness! What are those things with the long tails running around on top of our outside wall? Like big squirrels with long winding tails! Mom shouts, "Monkeys!" and laughs. I yip and woof and take off after them. Romie follows me in the fun. "Woo hoo! I'm gonna get you," I tease them. It sounds like they say back, "No you're not!" as they take off and scale the high fences and trees."

I nudge Romeo, "Did you see those guys? Their faces look like tiny humans! *Heh heh!*"

"Yeah, I see them all right. *Haha!*" Our bodies shake as we roll around on the lawn at the doggie humor.

Suddenly, we hear loud noises coming from the tree. "Chee chee chee!" I look up on the branch where there's a whole family of them. It feels like *they* are laughing at *us*! I get even more excited as I run in circles while barking at them. This is one of my most exciting days ever! A huge one is loping along from way across the lawn. We dash in his direction, screaming our heads off. Lots of fun! Especially after all those hours on the plane and in the car. They sneak down from the wall and the trees when we're not looking and tease us. We immediately take off to the other side of the yard to catch up with them. They are having as much fun as we are! Some have small babies that ride on their backs. They like to stare at us. Their little scheming faces look like they're always up to something. All my fatigue has vanished: I want to catch one so badly, but it's getting dark, so we must go inside.

First thing in the morning, we see a bunch of those monkeys from the window. The doors open, and we race out to the yard. The chase begins. They inch down close to us—as a tease. Sometimes, they linger on the grass eating a banana, looking like they own the yard. *Hmm,* maybe they do. I bark at them so much that they start *barking* back! I tell Romie, "I'm studying them to find their weak points, and one day they'll find out who they are messing with. *Heh heh!*"

Kate calls us back. Otherwise, I'm sure I could have caught one. Kate and Horace take us for a walk on the beach. It's only two short blocks away. It's so bright! It feels like we need doggie sunglasses! We get to the beach and it's covered with powdery white sand. We race off leash by the water's edge. Kate takes off her shoes and we all walk in the shallow water and feel the sand in our toes. It's not chilly like the Pacific Ocean. This is the Indian Ocean and it's clear and green with no big waves to knock us down. It's warm and feels good to our paws. The sand feels soft and the breeze is sweet. We prance through the sand, zigging and zagging several feet ahead of Mom, just having fun.

I don't notice the big brown wall up ahead. Suddenly, I am upon it and have to back up a bit. What is that smell? It reeks of wet animal hair. I go closer in for a sniff. Suddenly, the wall jerks and moves away from me. *Whoa!* A gigantic, exotic face turns from the other direction and, with its huge round eyes and sweeping eyelashes, glares at me face-to-face. I stand motionless as the two of us lock stares. His mouth is enormous, and I can see that *I would fit right in.* Although he's sitting down, I don't think I would be able to get away fast enough if he tried to eat me. I hope he won't squash me.

A local guy who is sitting in the sand, next to the camel, stands up. He chuckles and says, "Dat's Obama! Say hi!" Suddenly, Obama's gray tongue darts out and takes a lick of my head!

I bark. *Whoa!* His head is as big as my whole body. His tongue could wrap itself around me twice. If he really wanted to, I'm pretty sure he could eat me. He backs off from my bark. I hold my ground, and we have another staring contest. He chews on something and looks the other way. Now Obama is sitting and relaxed. I guess my touch didn't bother him too much.

Kate is rushing over. The young man says. "Ee won't hurt da dog. Ee sometimes gives rides to people and ee's very calm."

"That's good," says Kate. "Hi, Obama!" she chuckles. "Good thing he's a vegetarian and eats only leaves! Come on, Roxie, let's let Obama have his rest." Whew! Romie and I both run to Mom.

"Roxie, what did he smell like? Were you scared?" Romie asks.

"Not really. I could feel his calm energy and knew he wasn't going to eat me. I could smell grasses on his breath," I tell him.

This is something that we would never see on the beach in Santa Monica. Back home, they have a "no dogs allowed" policy on our beach. *Ha!* What about camels? *In your dreams!* I feel a little sorry for Obama since he has to do whatever the guy tells him and give rides. But so far, we haven't seen anyone riding him or his brothers.

***

Just then, we feel some sprinkles. "Right on time," says Kate. We're supposed to meet Roselyn at that little restaurant over there." She points to a beach motel and restaurant, right on the sand. Kate says she met Roselyn the last time she was in Africa and "Rosie" was going to help her find a job.

We all jog to the restaurant patio, jumping between the

raindrops. We stand close while Mom and Roselyn reunite. We like her right away. She has a musical voice and seems like she likes our mom a lot. "Hello, Roxie! Hi, Romeo! Let me give you a pet. You're so cute! Your mama told me all about you. I'm so happy to meet you." Her young daughter, Nikki, is with her, and she smiles at us. Luckily, she keeps her little fingers to herself, unlike some little kids who try to grab at us. "Hello, Horace, nice to meet you." Roselyn tells Kate that her professor from the university, Hari, is coming to join us.

We realize it's time for us to chill under the table and maybe catch a few scraps. So far, Africa is a really cool place. I'm liking it already.

Hari soon joins us all at the restaurant. He is also friendly but seems a little shy. He's not as boisterous as Roselyn. He is a teacher, but besides that, he helps run a home for young girls who have babies and they need some help. I hear Kate ask Hari what they teach the girls. He says, "They can learn a skill like hairdressing or tailoring, and how to take care of the baby. They usually don't go back to school, even though they had to drop out and didn't finish."

Kate says, "I'm hoping to find a job to help save elephants. I am very interested in saving wildlife and all of nature and helping people here appreciate the treasures of nature that surround them." She sweeps her hand toward the palm trees and the beautiful beach. "Why don't you teach the girls about wildlife conservation?"

He looks at her, a bit mystified.

"I notice this restaurant has plastic straws," Kate tells him, "and it's right on the beach. Plastic straws get in the ocean and can easily strangle and suffocate the marine life. This is a lesson on conservation, for example." And she pulls out of her purse a stainless-steel straw she got back home in Los Angeles.

"This metal straw is reusable. The girls could learn why it's important not to have plastic straws on the beach that harm sea life. The plastic doesn't dissolve but adds to the mountains of ocean garbage discarded by humans.

"The girls could learn how to get reusable straws wholesale by buying in bulk. And then they could learn how to talk to the restaurant owners and sell them the straws. That way, they could learn about business and, at the same time, help the environment and the ocean life—and earn money."

Hari is impressed with Kate. Who wouldn't be? She's very smart and nice and has good ideas. He asks, "Why don't you come and work for me?"

Kate says, "The reason why we came is to help elephants. I have a special fondness for them. Unfortunately, I don't believe there are many elephants around this area. That's the reason we are headed for Nairobi. I have some meetings with other conservationists and hoping they will help me get a job and a work permit."

He invites us all to go visit the home for the girls. "You can bring the dogs!" We're not that eager to go, and neither is Mom. We don't have that much time to spend in the town, and we want to go back to our yard and chase monkeys. But Hari is insistent. So we all end up piling in his car and taking a ride down the main road through the town. Then, we turn and go up a small dirt road—very bumpy and muddy—and get to the girls' home.

Kate is nervous because we pups are not used to being around young kids. She hasn't had a chance to train us for everything, you know. She knows that before I was rescued, when I used to stay in the yard, at times little kids would come and pull my hair. That's why I get nervous around kids and bark warnings at them. Romeo gets skittish around most strangers. Even though she has trained us both to behave as service dogs, Kate knows us well enough to realize that those old feelings can flare up.

When we get to the compound, Mom keeps us on a short

leash as we sniff around on the grounds. I notice a few little huts and an office. Lots of small kids running around. We all pose for a photograph and then Kate says we must get back to meet our driver Jackson. Hari drives us back. He tells Mom again that she could come and teach conservation to the girls. He says he can get her a work permit. She says she really appreciates it, but she already has plans to meet some elephant conservationists. She thanks him again and says they will stay in touch. Hari drives us back to our cottage and we say goodbye.

On the way back, we see a "Wayside Apartments – For Rent" sign near our rental house. Kate says, "Let's take a look, just for fun." It's for an apartment on the third floor of a building right near the beach. There are lots of monkeys in the yard.

We take a look at the apartment. It's spacious and has windows and patios everywhere. Lots of rooms. A large yard with trees and a big swimming pool. We all like it and could picture ourselves staying there. But we know we are leaving Diani Beach the next day. Mom tells the manager, "We will definitely keep it in mind if we come back to Diani."

The next morning, we leave with Jackson on our way to another part of Kenya where we'll stay. We hope it will be as much fun as the beach.

Chapter 3

ROMEO – Crocodiles

After we say goodbye to the monkeys and the beach, we drive toward our new home. Along the way, Jackson becomes our friend. He is a Maasai warrior and has grown up in the wild with his family and tribe, the Maasai people. Kate says they are among the very best people in Kenya who help preserve wildlife. Jackson likes us a lot and plays with us whenever he can. Kate is chatting with him in the front seat and we're in the back with Horace watching the scenery go by. The rest of the van is filled with our luggage. I feel so excited, almost as much as when I first met Kate and Roxie. Kate looks back at us and says, "There are lots of new things to learn about Kenya and Africa. When we first became a family, there were lots of things we had to all learn about each other. So now I want you to be alert and notice new things. Don't take things for granted. *I'm counting on you to help keep us all safe*," and she reaches back to give us both a rub.

I remembered when I used to be so excited all the time that it was hard for me to follow directions. Like when I picked up every piece of plastic I saw near the sidewalk and tried to eat it, just like I did when I was a hungry stray. Kate would pull it out of my mouth and say, "You don't want to eat that!" and then she would pop a little treat in my mouth. I'm not sure exactly what she means for us to do now, but I feel honored that she thinks we can help keep her safe.

After driving a few hours, Jackson asks us if we'd like to visit a snake and crocodile farm on the way. We don't know what that is, but Kate and Horace say okay, that it will be a nice break from the road. Soon, we're out of the van and walking among glass cages with all kinds of snakes inside. We've never seen such creatures. Some are sleeping in little circles, all coiled up. Others look at us and shoot out their long, skinny tongues. I jump back, in case the snake gets out and wants to bite us.

Kate warns us to be careful around critters in Africa, as there are lots of them that can bite us and hurt us "really bad." She says, "We must always stay away from these types of animals." We all stroll around and look at the lizards and bats.

We walk up a little hill along a fence. Jackson tells us that down the hill on the other side of the fence is where the big crocodiles live. On the other side of the fence we see critters that look like enormous lizards, only they have extra-long mouths with crooked teeth sticking out. The skin is all rough and bumpy. Their bellies are on the ground and they have long tails. Wow. I hope we don't see one of those in the wild—or on our side of the fence. Roxie leans in to have a look. Horace says crocodiles "could eat us for dinner." Gulp.

I notice a hole in the fence where it looks broken. It's a pretty big hole. Kate and Horace are talking to Jackson and don't notice it. Roxie is sniffing around near the back of our entourage.

As I look at Roxie, suddenly I spot *several* huge crocodiles slithering up the hill towards her. I yip. Roxie sees them, too, out the corner of her eye and barks in alarm. The crocs keep coming. We have to do something! Those crocodiles could eat us all! There's no time to warn Kate about the hole in the fence. Roxie yelps again, and we all turn. *There are hundreds of them, all crawling toward us!* She barks as they keep slithering quickly uphill. This time, I join her with a loud wolf howl. Her voice lifts to my volume and we sing as loudly as we can—as if our lives depend on it. Because they do!

Crazy as it sounds, our loud singing scares them away and the whole lot of them starts turning around and slithering back down the hill! Mommie and Grandpa laugh, and so does Jackson. Horace says to us, "You guys threw them in a panic, so they ran away." We feel proud. *Whew!* That was a close call! We keep watching as the crocodiles slink away on their little legs. Kate and Roxie and I look at each other and cheer.

Roxie and I have so many sounds we learned to make together. I couldn't help but remember that first time Mom showed us we could bark louder than the neighbor dogs who used to scare us. And then we practiced all the time to get on that television game show. When it was our turn to perform, that band started banging behind us. I ran like a crybaby behind Kate's legs.

But today, nothing can stop me and my loud voice from bellowing along with Roxie's. *And the crocodiles are terrified!*

They turn around and quickly slither back down the hill. We did it! We scared them away. I feel so proud. Vindicated. Maybe I couldn't win the TV contest, but I could scare crocodiles away! *Haha!* Kate, Horace and Jackson all laugh and clap.

But still, *they don't realize there is a hole in the fence*, or they may have started screaming at the top of their lungs, too. I realize it is *up to me* to show it to them. I jump up Jackson's legs and whimper. Then I look back towards the hole and whine. No one knows what I mean. But Kate says, "He's trying to show us something." They follow me, and they finally see the hole.

Jackson gets very serious. "Romeo, that's a good boy. Let's go and tell the manager what you found." We go to the office and find the manager. Jackson tells him there is a hole in the fence. The manager comes back with us to examine the hole. He looks at me with a serious look on his face. "What's his name?"

Mom says, "Romeo."

The manager says, "Romeo, that was a very good thing that you did. Nobody saw the hole until you came along, and you made sure to tell us about it—for the *safety of all*. That was a *great thing to do*. We will have the hole fixed right away so no one will have to fear the crocodiles getting through *because of you*."

Then everyone says, "Yay! Romeo! What a good boy! Yay!" and they all clap for me. That feels amazing. I'm not used to such praise. Usually *I* am the one who is screwing things up or nipping at the wrong people and have to be taught. I walk over to Roxie and rub against her. And they cheer, "Yay for Romeo and Roxie." I'm glad I did something good. How wonderful it must feel to be a real hero!

***

This acclaim brings back lots of old memories for me. I know for sure Mom and Horace and Roxie love me. But before they rescued me, almost no one had ever loved me or noticed me.

As we continue our drive and I am daydreaming in the car, I can't help but think about when I lived on the street and it felt like I was invisible to others. Even when I was put in the shelter, I was mostly ignored—except for that little boy Miguel. He was my very first love connection.

That shelter was a harrowing experience. When I was grabbed from the street by the dog catcher, I thought maybe it would be better than my life on the curb. At least I would be *inside*. Well, then I was inside, and I was offered some food every day. But I was still alone. Day and night. No one to see. Nothing to do. Still in pain. Nothing to take my mind off it. No fresh air. Nothing soft for my legs to be on. The shelter people decided no one would want me since I had handicaps. But they were wrong! There was that little boy who wanted me. He wanted me real bad. Miguel. So insistent. He wanted *me*. I needed a friend, and he needed a friend too.

One day, he came into the shelter with his mother. He ran over to *my* cage. *He liked me!* The boy yelled, "Mom! Look at this one. He's so cute. He has red spots! Let's take this one home!"

I put my snout through the bars and the boy rubbed my face. His fingers smelled like bananas. I felt my heart throbbing. "Ew! He stinks!" the mother said.

The little boy said, "I'll give him a bath! I promise. We can run and play after school. Please, Mama!" *Oh, I like this little boy!*

The mom said, "Let's get the attendant and see." They went to look for a shelter worker. I was hoping beyond hope they would take me out of the cage. I heard them walking back towards me.

The shelter lady was saying, "This one can't come out. He has something wrong with his legs."

I whimpered loudly. The little boy whined. "I want him! See—he wants to come home with us." *Oh, little boy, if you only knew how much I wanted to come!*

The lady said to the mom, "He won't be able to run. You'll have to take him to a vet, and maybe one or both of his legs are broken. He can barely walk."

The boy cried. The mom said, "Miguel, you wouldn't be able to run with him. His leg is broken."

Miguel said, "Why don't they get his leg fixed?"

The shelter lady said, "We're just a poor small shelter with too many dogs. We don't have enough money to fix up every stray who comes in here. At least we give them food and shelter for a while and someone might come along who wants to take them home."

Miguel screamed, "We could get it fixed!"

I wailed with Miguel. I howled and howled as he cried. He must have been very lonesome, too. I tried to kiss him through the bars. I felt sorry that he was so lonesome he wanted a broken dog like me.

The mom said, "I'm sorry, Miguel. We don't have the extra money to go to the vet. And then, suppose we *did* go to the vet? The dog would have to be in a bandage for a long time, so he still couldn't run with you."

Miguel cried louder.

The shelter lady said, "Let's go look at some other doggies."

Miguel cried, "I want this one!"

My heart was breaking for this little boy. I felt that *I could make him so happy, if they would only let me try!*

The two ladies pulled him, kicking and screaming, away from my pen. I howled and wailed as I heard Miguel being pulled farther and farther away. Then, I put my head down and wept.

The next day, I heard people coming in. I pulled myself up to the bars and waited there. *Maybe they won't notice my sore legs.* A lady and man walked down the long hall. They looked at me. I tried to look hopeful and gave them a friendly bark. I could smell an animal smell on them. Maybe a cat. The lady looked closely at a plaque on my cage.

"Special needs. Damaged legs. Oh, too bad. He's a cute one. Hello in there! Oh dear, we'd better not get his hopes up. Bye, bye, doggie."

I howled and cried, then I got very still.

***

I open my eyes to a big jolt. Our van goes over a hole in the road and it balks. I am suddenly thrown from my reverie. I take a deep breath. I look around. I remember I am in Africa! I am surrounded by my loving Roxie and my wonderful mom, Kate, and Horace. I'm no longer alone. I breathe deeply.

I look in Roxie's eyes and say, "I'll never forget the day I met you and Kate at the door. Kate had found my photo and wanted to meet me. You guys were as ecstatic to see me as I was to see you. For the first time in my life, someone really wanted me. Both human and dog. *It was the luckiest day of my life.* You've taught me how to be part of a family and to be loved. But today in Africa is the very *first time I could do something good for others*, too. It makes me proud."

I never expected this to happen in Africa. I didn't think I could ever be happy anywhere besides my long-sought-after home. But maybe coming to a new land with new animals is good. Here, we are all new and we can experience life together. I want to be someone that my family can count on, whom they could be proud of. Here, it feels like there are new possibilities. Everyone says I'm a hero today.

For the first time in my life, a trickle of confidence pours through me. Maybe *when it really counts, I come through.*

Chapter 4

ROMEO – Our Friend the Elephant

The road trip to Nairobi is hours and hours. I am feeling restless again. Mom says we'll spend the night at a lodge on the way, where we might be able to see some wild animals. Roxie and I look at each other, hopeful.

Suddenly, I hear Kate say to Jackson, "Stop! Please stop! I want to take a picture of that *elephant*." I look out the window, and I see an elephant some distance away on the side of the road. He looks just like the elephant statues we have back home. I want to go closer and say hi, but the driver says the traffic is bad and he can't stop. We keep going.

About an hour later, we finally stop. We get out of the car and stretch. We walk towards a huge building. We look around for monkeys but don't see any. After Kate and Horace check in, we stroll with Kate towards the spacious outdoor patio where they serve dinner. We are excited and want to run around, but we have to stay close.

Right outside the patio somewhere, there's a place Mommie calls a *waterhole* where wild animals come and get a drink of water. We're looking around for it in all directions. We see an animal moving—and it is *gigantic!* We go closer, quietly, to see what it is.

"It's an *elephant!*" Roxie exclaims.

From the patio fence, he's only a few feet away. We stop dead in our tracks and stare. The elephant stares back at us. He's pulling in water through his long trunk and putting it in his mouth. We don't bark or anything. We stand in awe of the elephant. He is the biggest animal we have ever seen. He looks at us, and we look at him, and he keeps drinking water. We pull hard on our leashes to get a better view. Then Mom and Roxie and I all tiptoe in his direction.

He's brownish and looks like Mom's statues and pictures.

Whoa! I never could have imagined an animal that enormous. Not only that, but he is calm and peaceful as he is drinking water. We are all awe-struck. We stand perfectly still. This animal is so massive, if he wanted to, he could probably tear the whole building down! But his spirit is like a gentle and sweet song of a small bird. We hear the sound of the water being sucked in all the way up his long pipe of a trunk. Though he is a gazillion times our size, we don't feel nervous at all.

He keeps looking at us. He smells of green grasses, salty hay, and rich mud. We feel his strong energy coming our way. It makes me feel warm and secure. It feels like *love*. Roxie and I are both feeling serene and joyous in his presence. We check in with each other with our eyes sparkling.

The elephant keeps drinking and flapping his giant ears. We catch a breeze from those flaps. We feel his curiosity about us as he conveys to us strong, loving energy. It's as though time stands still. Suddenly, he takes a huge swig of water and raises his long trunk up to the sky. And his huge ivory tusks sweep down halfway to the ground.

Mom whispers, "He's a bull elephant. At one time, these huge animals used to roam the whole earth! Not just the countries of Africa, but all over the world, even back in California." I keep watching him and imagining all the elephants walking all over the earth. I look up at Mom. She says, "These are the last of the elephants. Today, there are herds left in only a few countries. Isn't he magnificent?" She is gaping and seems totally immersed in our elephant friend. "This is why we came here. We must help save the ones who are left." It's hard for me to imagine saving a big animal like this, especially since I am so small. I would *like* to imagine that I am brave and fearless. I wish I could have friends like this handsome big guy.

The elephant keeps staring at us. There is gentleness, even in his stare. I stare back. I feel the same kind of energy I felt when I met Kate. It's like a vibrating love bond, a magnetic force. I glance at Roxie and see that she is staring and feeling it too. Our eyes are glued on the elephant. He takes another long swoop of water. We've been traveling all day and are dry. We lick our lips automatically when we see all that fresh water.

He takes another swoop, lifts his trunk up high, then shoots the water up in the air. It makes a long rainbow arc aimed toward us. The water's pouring down towards us above our heads. I look up, gaping and the stream goes right into my mouth. The elephant is giving me a drink! Then he does the same for Roxie. I can't believe it. We slurp the elephants' water. It's like he can read our minds! It's the best tasting water I ever drank!

Being near the elephant makes me feel serene—and also strong, like I imagine I would feel if he were part of my family. It's like he's imparting some of his energy and power to me. He makes me *feel* like an elephant, like I am starting to *become* more "elephant!"

Mom says, "We are all one family on earth. All the animals

and people are connected." I am rapturous. I howl at the top
of my lungs. Roxie joins in and we are singing our duet to the
elephant. The elephant makes a loud trumpeting noise back at
us and with us. We look at each other and carry on. *The
elephant is singing with us!* It's the most beautiful sound in
the world. Kate howls, too. A moment to cherish. My core is
shaking. Mom hugs us both and we feel so close to her. Time
stands still. I love elephants. Now I have an elephant friend.
Now I know why we came to Africa.

A waiter comes rushing over to us. He tells Kate to not
allow her dogs to disturb the elephant. Mom says we are *not
disturbing him*, but we were *all singing together*. The waiter
frowns. Anyway, Kate says, we must find Horace and get back
to our room. I see the elephant is walking away from the
waterhole. Soon we are walking away too.

One existential moment can change everything. Kate has
told us about the baby elephants and how she felt they were
communicating with their minds. I wasn't sure what she
meant, but now I completely understand. I want to help
elephants, too. I love my Kate and Horace. I love Roxie. I love
all the animals. And most of all, I love elephants.

Nighttime, and my head is still full of elephant thoughts. I
can barely sleep.

Elephant! You are an elephant!
You are so big, and I am so small,
Your heart is so grand—You make me feel tall.
You are my friend, I feel loved by you,
I won't be the same 'cause your love is true.
Now and forever, I'll be just like you,
Inspired by you,
You're my animal family, too.

The next morning, we have to get back in the van to
continue our drive to Nairobi. We don't see the elephant again.

I keep an eye out for any other elephants that might be on

the road, but I don't see any. I close my eyes and daydream some more. I'm sure Roxie is daydreaming too. Every so often, I hear her snort. When I look at her, she is smiling in her dreams.

Chapter 5

ROXIE – Our New Home

We drive and drive and drive. Finally something is different. A smell of smog in the air. The sound of cars and trucks, and pedestrians talking loudly. We must have gotten to a city. Here, the air has a chill to it. Jackson tells us that the Maasai name for Nairobi is "place of cool waters." I get up on my haunches and look out the car window at the traffic. The bright sunshine we felt earlier on our trip has disappeared, and the whole sky looks gray. It feels chilly. We thought Africa would be warmer.

We drive by a pretty, wooded area and then a street where everyone's house is hiding behind a tall fence and gate. The van stops. Mom calls out, and a lady named Mrs. M comes to let us in the driveway. It feels great to get out of the van. There are a few houses behind the gate. We go to ours which is the first one with its own small fence and gate and we go inside. This is our yard.

"Wow! I say, "Look at this."

Romie agrees. "Roxie! This is as big as a park! We have our own private park!"

Mrs. M says her mother used to live here and she

cultivated lots of flowers and plants. We take off running up and down the hilly yard, dashing around plants and trees. Heaven! We hear some loud bird sounds. We look up. Way high in a tree is a big nest and a bird is spreading her massive wings and looking down at us. She must be three times our size. I have the uncomfortable feeling she could pick us up with her huge talons and bring us up to her nest if she wanted to. We find out later she is a golden eagle.

As we are sniffing every inch of the yard, another gigantic bird with a long, straight beak lands in the middle of our lawn. She struts confidently as if she owns the place. She's at least twice as big as us and she doesn't seem at all bothered by us. I bark in her direction but she ignores me. Kate tells us she is an ibis. I am about to ambush her, when we are quickly distracted by a chattering in a tall tropical tree in another part of the yard.

We look up, and we see a huge monkey, bigger than those at the beach. I lead the charge, and we run up to the tree and give him a good bark. Romeo does his wolf howl. The monkey screeches loudly as he hops sloppily to another treetop, barely noticing us.

Just as we are getting to feel like lord and lady of the mansion, we hear loud dog barking. The landlady's three German Shepherds and two Jack Russell terriers are suddenly glaring at us from the other side of the fence. Uh oh. We cringe. Mom calls us to the door. We take off running in her direction. Suddenly, being in our own park doesn't seem so private. Obviously there are plenty of other creatures who consider this yard to be *their* territory.

Kate and Horace are talking with the landlady inside the house when a tall fellow with a bellowing voice pops in through the door. Romeo barks at him ferociously. Kate tells Romie to "calm down." It's Mrs. M's husband. Something about him is odd. Romeo can't stop barking. He feels it's his job to warn our parents of dangerous people. The guy comes inside and speaks loudly with a strange accent. Romeo can't stop growling. Mom tells him again to stop. He muffles himself but he's still growling under his breath. The guy acts like he doesn't hear Romeo and keeps ranting on with his loud voice. Finally, Mrs. M says, "We'd better let you be. I know you have a lot of unpacking to do." At last. Now we could explore our cavernous digs.

It is becoming evening and I notice it is downright chilly inside the house. This is something else we didn't expect. We hadn't realized before that, in California, we were used to central heating. When we got cold, all we had to do was turn up the heat, and in a few minutes the whole house was warm. Here, there is no central heating. We go to the back of the house where the bedrooms are. It is even colder back there. It's a good thing we stopped on the way and got some food. Otherwise we would be pretty hungry. The refrigerator is bare. The house is cold. The big dogs are at the gate. All we want to do is get under the covers.

The next day is even grayer and cooler. We're grumpy. Horace rounds up some wood from the men who work on the grounds. He lights a small, smoky fire in the fireplace. The air in the living room becomes thick. In the back of the house, it is still ice cold.

When Kate takes us out for a walk, we pass by dozens of monkeys who are staring down at us from our roof, the fence, and the bushes. They aren't playing with each other or teasing us like they did at the beach. They look surly. Some of the little white-and-gray monkeys have mischievous looks on their faces. Kate says they are vervets. And there are dark gray ones that are twice their size—much bigger than us! Those are called Sykes.

Later, I see the vervets look into the kitchen window from the other side of the house. Imagine looking up at your Mom and seeing behind her, peeking in the window, a silly monkey face! We know we're not in California anymore! Maybe this will be a jolly place to live, after all. I try to be optimistic.

We see more huge birds, much larger than we are, prancing around our yard. It's like a fantasy land. They seem slow, but when we try to chase them, they easily take flight.

We are hoping that the next-door dogs will lighten up because we miss having dog friends around. But they don't like us too much. Actually, not one bit. They appear opposite the fence and gape at us with teeth bared and hatred in their eyes. They all bark at us at the same time, and the sound of it sends chills. The Jacks act brave—as if they have their own personal guard dogs. I have never met dogs before who looked at me like I am prey.

That night at bedtime, I think about the dogs. I hope Kate realizes they could be difficult for us to deal with. I am reminded of my experience with Marcello. He was a much nicer dog than these are, but he could also be a bully. Kate loved him so much she didn't always see his meanness coming out. I had to defend myself.

I lie in my traveling dog bed and give that a thought. When I was a new member of the family, Marcello was used to being the total object of adoration. Most of the time he was calm, but dinnertimes were another story. Marcello would gobble up everything in his bowl. Then he'd look at me and my bowl, and he'd growl loudly with a mean look on his face. This made me more squeamish about food than I already was. Even though I generously let him have all the chewies, he still turned into a werewolf at dinnertime.

Kate told him, "Stop growling!" But did he listen? No.

In matters of food, he only listened to his inner cravings.

I just had to do *something*, so I made a plan. I had to psych myself up—as my strategy was a new behavior for me. Rumor had it that some boy dogs don't fight with girl dogs, and I was banking on that being true. Next time he growled at me, I'd jump on him and show him who was boss. I wasn't sure how that was going to work, but I just had to do something.

Dinnertime. He scarfed down his food while I was still enjoying mine piece by piece. I paced myself and waited for his snarl. Here it comes!

Whop! I jumped on him—he fell over, just like that! It was almost too easy. *Heh heh!* I couldn't stop there. Even though he had at least eight pounds on me, I stayed on top of his belly, yipping at his face. He didn't fight back. My theory was correct.

Kate and Gerard stared in disbelief.

I'm not an aggressive dog. *But*, I told myself, *a girl can be pushed only so far. I lived with this bully and put up with his growls every day. I had a right to take action.* Finally, I laid off and slowly ate my food. Marcello didn't say much. At least he was gentleman enough to refuse to fight with a warrior princess!

I knew I'd have to repeat this scenario more than once to get the message through his thick skull. I jumped on him the next day at dinner when he growled. The day after that, I jumped on him when he even looked mean. The next time he so much as looked at me out the corner of his eye, I was on top of him again, nipping at his face.

Marcello protested, "All right! All right, already! You made your point!" He headed for a corner, and sulked. *He never did it again. Heh heh! Goes to show you, girl power!*

After our bouts, Kate checked that Marcello was all right, and I guess he was, because I didn't get any reprimands. She said she was proud of me for sticking up for myself. She added that I had trained Marcello to be a gentleman, *whereas she wasn't able to.* I began to see that sometimes Kate *needs me* to help her. This made me feel more at home, since *I need to help those who I love.* It's just who I am.

In the case of our growling neighbor dogs, I wonder why the Shepherds hate us. Is it because we have such a great yard? They have a large yard, too, yet they try to sneak into ours, or they hunker at the gate and scowl at us or holler their heads off.

As it turns out, every day we are there, Romeo digs up one or two bones from our yard. Mom won't let us chew on them, though, and she puts them all in a bucket. Maybe the dogs are mad because we have all their bones in our yard. But *they* are the ones who buried them—right where we could find them.

And that isn't the only problem. The people next door act like our house is theirs, too, and they stop by a lot. At home in California, people don't usually pop in when you don't know they are coming. Here, it feels like an invasion. They are always telling Kate what to do. Sometimes it's good, because we really need to understand how people behave here, but mostly it's unpleasant. Kate says she'll walk us down to the coffee shop—but the landlady says "*No!* It's dangerous. People can rob you!" Kate wears a small elephant necklace. The landlady tells her, "*No!* You do not want to do that. Someone will steal it."

Kate asks, "Right off my neck?"

The landlady nods firmly as she replies, "They'll know you're new around here and they may try to take advantage." She tells Kate to stop wearing her bracelets. Mom has pretty bracelets, especially her new blue one from Tanzania. She doesn't like to be told these things. Later, I see her take off her jewelry before leaving the house.

Kate tells Horace that Mrs. M is an alarmist, but on the other hand, we need to be cautious since we don't know the area. Jackson visits us occasionally but is not with us now, and we don't have a car anymore, so we are a little stuck. Mom walks us up and down our one street and another street nearby. We are both game for meeting some new dog friends. But at the same time, we're on the lookout for someone who may try to steal something. If we need to go a farther distance, she calls a driver.

Hardly anyone else is out walking on our lonely road. Occasionally, we see a woman with a big basket or bundle on her head. Kate looks in amazement. She smiles and says, "Hi," in a faint voice with no response. It makes it seem even more lonely. All the houses are hidden behind the tall fences. When we pass nearby their barricades, we can hear loud barking and ferocious warnings behind the walls. We don't see anybody out walking dogs on leashes. The occasional person we do see looks at us and stares. What kind of place did we end up in, anyway? How could we fit into this unfriendly place? By the time we come back from our walk, the sky is still gray and the air cool. It's uncomfortably cold in the house. I feel gloomy. Maybe we will feel better when the sun comes out.

In the days that follow, Kate is on the phone a lot. Jackson introduces us to Rhoda and her daughter, Val, two nice ladies who do some cleaning and cooking. We like their company, and Val especially enjoys us, but both of them seem shy and not used to being around little dogs. I am always friendly, but Romie is more cautious and usually sits back so I try to be extra nice.

Truth is, I don't think Romeo really knows how to be hospitable. He never bonded with anyone before Kate and me. He always felt on his guard around humans. I guess those feelings don't go away overnight. Or even after months. I wonder if they ever go away.

Jackson sometimes drives us. Other times, Mom calls a taxi. We get car rides to the store. Once, we had to wait in the car while Kate and Horace shopped for supplies. We don't mind staying with Jackson, but with a new driver, we would feel uncomfortable. Suppose he took us away while they were in the store?

There is one driver we start to get familiar with named Charles. He likes us and is curious about our lifestyle. He has never seen two dogs get toted around in the car all the time with their own little dog beds to keep them comfortable. Kate does not waste an opportunity to regale him with stories and lessons about how dogs are part of the family. "Dogs are intelligent and have feelings and attachments," she tells him. "They like to be with their humans." Romie and I always smile at each other when she says things like this, and when possible we cozy up to her, our beloved parent and caretaker.

As far as dogs in our hood, we still never see a dog or meet anyone walking one—not for days and weeks. One day, we see a dog behind her gate who doesn't appear to be angry. We go close to the gate to say hello, but she is too timid to interact with us. We go back to her gate many times looking for her to say hello, but she isn't there. When we finally see her again, she still acts fearful. It's sad that none of these dogs are friendly. I wonder if any of them have ever had another dog for a friend.

Our walks get more humdrum as we hardly see anybody and never any other dogs. We can only walk in a limited area. A guy passes by in a car and  asks Kate, "How much do you want for them?" We soon realize they are talking about *us*! Stupid guy! As if Mommie would ever sell us! *Haha!* That's funny. But later I start to wonder: *She won't ever sell us, will she? How much would we cost?* I know Kate loves me, but just thinking about it makes me blue.

A different guy drives by in a big car. He pulls over right next to us. He says to Kate, "How much you want for them?"

Mom is as startled as we are. "They're not for sale."

"Are you breeding them? Will you have puppies for sale?"

Mom answers, "No. They are pets."

"You mean you are walking them around, but you're not selling them or their puppies?"

"I mean they are not having any puppies and they are my pets. Like my children."

The man's eyes widen. He makes a funny sound. Then he pulls away rather abruptly.

I look at Romie. "They want to buy us!"

Romeo says, "I wonder how much we're worth."

Kate looks at us and sees we look confused. "I would never sell you. Roxie and Romeo, you are my babies. Forever!" She reaches down to give us a hug. We smile at each other and rub against her. "We love you too, Mommie!"

We go back in the house. She tells Horace, "A guy wanted to buy the dogs!"

He says, "Well, they're not for sale."

I wonder why somebody around here would want us. We're pretty small to be watchdogs. Romeo says, "When I was living on the street and also in the pound, nobody wanted me, not even for free. I had to stay in the foster homes for months while my legs were healing, but as far as I know, no one even considered keeping me. That is, until I met you and Kate and we all fell in love. That was the best day of my life. So it seems ironic that someone wants to pay money for us now."

I say, "It makes me wonder what's on these peoples' minds? What would they do with us, anyway?" We both take a big sigh and go lie down on the patio to contemplate our situation.

Romie says, "You know how Kate told us to be proud to be terriers, because terriers have a reputation for being courageous and spunky? Well, I think Kate may be a terrier, too!"

"Yes! You're absolutely right. Our terrier mom!" We both sputter and snort. "She told those guys where it's at!" I tell him.

"That's why she's the best mom ever!" he adds. We roll around on the old carpet in the living room and ease into our afternoon naps.

One day, a few weeks later, Charles tells us his son has found a dog on the street and brought her home. Kate congratulates him for allowing this. The next day, when she goes to the store, she brings him a dog bed and a collar and leash for the dog. She tells us later, "You are wonderful role models for the people and dogs we meet. When people see how well behaved you are and how much you can share with your humans, it helps them get some new ideas." Romie and I look at each other out of the corners of our eyes and smile.

Chapter 6

ROMEO – Roxie's Know-How

Roxie reminds me that it's our job to stay alert to the monkeys and the next-door dogs—not to mention watching for the landlords and scouting for baboons. She says, "Kate and Horace are depending on us to help keep everyone out of trouble."

Monkeys hover around the kitchen window. I'm not sure if they can sneak inside, but Roxie wants to forewarn them it is not allowed. They always bring their troupe with them. They sit on a nearby bush eating flowers while blithely peering in our kitchen window. Others sit on the roof and look down at us as we go out the door. She is determined to catch one so "they'll know who controls our yard!"

One day, Kate has some appointments and Charles escorts her out in the morning. We stay at home with Horace. He doesn't enjoy walking us like Mom does. He opens the kitchen door and lets us go in the small yard in the front by the kitchen. Those inquiring monkeys are perched in their usual places on the fence and top of the house, which is a bit creepy. I opt to stay inside.

Roxie goes sniffing outdoors. Before she knows it, one of the monkeys jumps down and lands on top of her. Horace and I hear the squabble from inside. We hear a monkey sound and then snaps and growls from our Roxie. Horace looks out the kitchen window and sees them tussling. He runs outside and yells, 'Go away!'"

That's when the monkey takes off. Horace picks Roxie up and brings her inside.

"That little squirt jumped right on top of me! He was laughing and pulling my hair. Like he thought I was some toy to play with. Just like those little kids who used to tease me before Kate adopted me. It made me so mad. The monkey was small but his fingers were strong. He threw me off my game. How dare he? I will find him sometime and teach him a lesson," she says.

I tell her, "Roxie, suppose that monkey's mother came after you too? That would be scary!"

"I know," she says, "but you have to defend yourself. You have to fight for what's right. I learned that when I was a puppy. Rex was sick and I had to stick up for him just to survive."

I say, "That's the first time ever I saw you get upset."

I cuddle up right next to her to help her calm down. Secretly, I am also hoping that no monkey ever jumps on *me*. I don't know what I would do. I am good at being snarly and acting mean around humans, but I have a feeling that another animal would be able to see right through that act and know I am a scaredy cat.

When we stayed at Diani Beach, nobody was upset when they saw monkeys. And there were lots of them. But for some reason, around here, there seems to be more fear and dislike between people and monkeys. Later, we hear Kate and Horace talking. Kate says, "We are living right on the edge of a forest, perhaps the animals think the area is all their terrain and don't like humans living close by—let alone dogs! Maybe when people first built the house, it was still animal territory, and they haven't forgotten. Horace says, "Besides that, Mrs. M told us that no one was living in the house for a long time before we came, and the monkeys and neighbor dogs must have had the run of the place."

All the animals look at us as though *we* are the invaders. And in a way, we *are*. At least the monkeys near the doorway aren't that big. These smaller vervet monkeys are the comical ones, trying to peek into the windows and such. I say, "Roxie, you and I have a similar sense of humor for sure. I love to tease you, too. But this time, I'm not sure what got you so shook up. You didn't see the humor in it and somehow felt humiliated by that little monkey. Tell me, how exactly did it happen? What was going through your mind?"

Roxie replies, "A monkey jumped down from the fence, right on top of me, and we tussled like two lightweight wrestlers I saw on television. His long, thin arms were able to enclose me. I dug at his chest like it was sand. I was shocked by my own fierce reaction—my instincts kicked in. I thought about Marcello and how I jumped on *him* that time. *What would Marcello do now?* He wasn't afraid of anyone—except me, when I beat him up. *Heh heh!* That's right, Marcello *didn't dare fight me back.* All these crazy thoughts were rushing through my brain as my heart was thumping.

"I wasn't going to let this cheeky monkey make a fool of me. He'd be sorry he ever jumped on me! As we kept rolling and pulling on the ground, I noticed he was smaller than most. It's possible he was just a baby. I did shiver when I had the thought that his family could come after me.

"Horace saw us through the window and came running out. He shouted at the monkey and frightened him away. *Whew!* I felt relieved. I wondered what would've happened if he *didn't* see us. Maybe the next time he won't come out—and I'll have to fight on my own. I have to admit that I was shaken and not at all prepared. Next time I'll have to be ready."

After that, Roxie keeps a keen lookout for the little squirt. One day she spots him looking down from our rooftop. But for many weeks, he never jumps on her again—nor does any other monkey come close enough for Roxie to pounce on him. I tell her, "I guess you showed them who's boss, warrior princess!"

We chase the larger monkeys in the backyard, though they are swinging from high trees and not paying us much mind. Gradually, they become like part of the landscape, and we all keep our distance.

The neighbors' dogs, though, are a different story, and they still act malicious. The German Shepherds try to sneak up and frighten us, and the Jacks do, too, but only when they have their entourage. It turns out those Jack Russell terriers are wimps. After we have been here a few weeks, we see one of them sniffing around on the grounds by himself. Kate calls to him sweetly to say hello. Even though we are on leashes, as we walk closer, the Jack takes off in the opposite direction and dives into the bushes. Scared to death of us!

The dogs around here do not know how to enjoy life.

Chapter 7

ROXIE – Is Kate an Elephant?

One of Kate's mentors is passing through town and we're looking forward to having lunch with her. We get to go with Kate to the restaurant patio on the other side of the woods. She brings our dog beds along and we know we must behave. She told us about Joyce back in California. Joyce lives with elephants in the forests and plains and studies their communication. She's studied them a long time and observed their every sound and movement.

Joyce started an organization called ElephantVoices, and it's known all over the world! Whenever elephants make different moves with their trunks or different kinds of noises, Joyce makes notes, snaps photos, and tapes a video recording. She says the elephants are often talking to each other. They can even send messages to their friends who are far away. Sometimes, they make sounds that travel underneath the earth. They can feel them with the soft pads in their feet.

Romie and I are excited. We're thinking *she must study elephants the way we do, just like dogs study humans.* We canines learn about humans and what they want and how they feel by studying their every move. That's the same thing Joyce does with elephants! We can't wait to see what she looks like. We wonder if she has a keen nose like we do, or maybe her ears will be like ours and stand up so she can hear things far away. We feel sure we'll see *something* about her that's like a dog.

When Joyce arrives, Romie and I both examine her closely. She is a very sweet, soft-spoken, and nice-looking woman, and we can't detect anything different about her looks. Her ears, eyes, and nose all look like a standard human's. We love her anyway. She encourages Kate in finding a great job working with elephants. She shows us pictures of Binti, her cute Shepherd dog. We learn that Joyce is the one who told Kate how to get us safely into Kenya by going through Tanzania. *And* she brings us little treats for under the table. We're sure that Kate would have liked to work with Joyce, but Joyce says she is now "staying in Europe for a sabbatical."

Kate invites people over for dinner. The guests like playing with me because I make them feel welcome, even when we don't know them very well. If they're good enough for Kate and Horace, they're good enough for me. Mom says I am the official greeter. It's fun. Romeo is more cautious, especially with new people. But I always know he has my back.

Sammy is a caretaker with baby elephants. The baby elephants are all alone because their mothers have died or they got lost or sick, so the babies need humans to take care of them. Kind of like dogs, I guess. It's awesome to meet people who spend their whole lives taking care of elephants. We don't know anyone like that back in California. Sammy lets me climb up on his chest and give him kisses on his face. I wonder if the elephants do that to him, too. Later Mommie says they do!

Kate visits the orphanage at the Sheldrick Wildlife Trust where Sammy works. She loves to visit her adopted Enkesha and Ngilai along with the other baby elephants. She has been hoping to get a job there at Sheldrick's, but there aren't any openings. At first, she wanted to be a caretaker, but Edwin, the head caretaker, told her that to get that job you have to be big and strong. The baby elephants usually weigh over two hundred pounds, and the caretaker has to be able to corral them when necessary. Kate is a petite woman. It's a good thing Romeo and I are less than twenty pounds each. She can corral us really good.

We can't go with her to meet Enkesha and Ngilai—they don't allow dogs into the nursery or stockades where the elephants are. This is a big disappointment for us. Some of the nature films we watch with her are about the Sheldrick Wildlife Trust. And sometimes, Mom shows us cool videos she's taken there of the elephants. Sometimes, though, they're on her cell phone, and they're hard for us to see.

Daphne Sheldrick founded the orphanage when she was young. She loved animals, especially elephants, and started rescuing all the orphans she could find. There were wild animals who lost their mothers, or the mother was killed or even died from illness. Daphne helped the orphans so they could go back into the wild and live free. She didn't try to keep them for pets or anything.

An elephant would be a big pet to have. Nobody would have enough room for them. And they would be lonesome without seeing other elephants. Just like I was lonesome when I couldn't find Rex or have a home—until I got adopted by Kate and Gerard and met Marcello. Before Marcello and I became friends, I was lonesome. I missed Rex and someone to play with. Marcello was so much older than me. I think I was about a year old and he was around thirteen. Like hanging out with your great-grandfather. *Heh heh!*

When Kate first took us to a march for elephants in L.A., she was telling me all about elephants, and I was wondering if she and Gerard might adopt an elephant like they adopted me. I knew they were big, but I had no idea *how* big. I was wondering where one would sleep. Would she have to have a special elephant bed?

One night, I dreamt that an elephant was my playmate. We'd go on walks around the neighborhood. I'd run between the elephant's legs and climb up her trunk. She'd flap her ears to keep me cool. We were best friends. We'd roll around in the living room, both chirping happily. I started rolling in my sleep and I rolled right off the big bed! *Plop!* I landed smack on top of Marcello in his dog bed! Half-asleep, I thought he was the elephant, and I kissed him. He snarled. I held my breath, but then he closed his eyes and went right back to sleep. I tiptoed away! I think Mommie was watching me with one eye closed. I heard her giggling to herself.

Kate enjoys talking to the caretakers. Especially Sammy. He is so mellow. This is the first time I ever heard her say how *she herself may have been an elephant!* Romie and I could hardly believe it! Kate told Sammy, "Many years ago, I experienced a phenomenon that is called a 'past life regression' in a doctor's office." She said, "The doctor helped people with their problems by hypnotizing them to make them feel relaxed. Then, when the patient was almost asleep, that's when they could explore what was deep in their minds. I was a pretty young woman at the time. I was very relaxed in a chair with my eyes closed. The doctor guided me to explore what happened when I was one year younger, then another year younger, back further and further until my little pinky finger would pop up automatically, he said, and I would remember something important. In my case, nothing happened when I traveled back in time even to my childhood. The doctor kept saying different ages and it got down to 'five, four, three, two, one...' and nothing happened. Then he said 'zero' and suddenly my pinky finger popped up!

"I had a vivid experience as a young orphan in Africa whose mother was killed by a hunter. I was very frightened and alone as I raced through the jungle to escape. I came upon a herd of peaceful elephants. The elephants welcomed me and took care of me. After that, I lived happily in the jungle with them. They became my family." Kate continues, "It felt very real to me—like I was living through every moment right there in the office. I cried and screamed—it seemed to come out of nowhere. I had never been to Africa before, I didn't know much about elephants—I hadn't ever *seen* one up close, and certainly wasn't even *thinking* about elephants!"

Later she told her friends about the experience. Eventually, she stopped musing about it. "But about ten years later," Kate says, "I developed a burning desire to have a dog, and I adopted Marcello. We had such a strong bond. That made me realize how much I love dogs, and that I have always loved dogs—back to the time I had Bernie, even though I only had him for a short time as a young girl. I learned all I could about dogs, and I discovered that many of them need rescuing. I began helping dogs and other animals. I started writing about animals in a news journal. I met my wildlife photographer husband, Gerard, and we worked on wildlife articles together in Africa. I met animal advocates and elephant researchers and I became a total animal activist. Now elephants are my passion (besides Roxie and Romie, that is!)." As she says this to Sammy, she winks over at us.

Romeo loves that story. He says to me, "Is it possible to live another lifetime? I would have never thought of that. But it's a mind-blowing idea. That way people and animals who have a terrible life might be able to have a wonderful life next time!"

I tell him, "We may not ever know for sure if we have another life—even Kate, after she went through that experience, she says she's not sure what to make of the vision."

Sammy is mesmerized by her story. So are we pups. We just can't get enough.

"When I was touring on one of my trips to Africa," she says, "I meditated and wrote poetry and felt inspired. I came to believe that in my past life, maybe *my mother wasn't a human, but an elephant*. If so, I may have *been* a baby elephant! No one has ever heard of elephants raising a human child, but they could rescue a baby elephant, especially if they may be related to her mother. It's all very mysterious."

Romeo says, "If Mom was an elephant, I wonder if we could have been part of her elephant family? Maybe we were elephants, too!"

I ask, "And we somehow have all found each other again?"

Romie says, "Maybe!" He pauses, then adds, "Why should only cats have nine lives, after all? *Haha!*"

I snort, "Maybe I'll see you in your next life, too!"

"I hope so!" Romie says.

***

Kate frequently talks to her Kenyan friends on the phone or has them visit. It seems they are all trying to help her find a job working with elephants. She discovers that visitors are not allowed by the Kenyan government to stay in the country for more than a few months without a work permit.

She leaves us for a few days to visit some of her acquaintances in the "bush." Friends of hers in the Maasai Mara wants her to work with their projects. She says they showed her a house where we could all live. It was nice but situated right in the midst of the jungle surrounded by hundreds of big wild animals like elephants, lions, cheetahs and rhinos. She says she realized there was no place to walk us dogs. There wasn't even a fence around it. Some of the wild animals might try to eat us. Without a car, we would be trapped in the jungle.

Romeo and I feel bad that she is giving up a fun job because of us. I hope she won't regret bringing us to Africa. We decide we'll both look for a way to make her feel happy she brought us.

On another trip, she leaves town to meet with Hari about the job in Diani Beach. There are no elephants nearby, but she thinks maybe she could be helpful there to the girls and still help elephants. But right now, things are up in the air.

***

One afternoon, we are napping in the living room when we hear Mrs. M screaming. "Baboons! Get the dogs inside! Baboons!"

We're already inside, so we wonder what all the commotion is about. We spotted some baboons before when we were leaving Diani Beach. They look like big strong monkeys. Mrs. M told Mom they could come after us and steal our bags or do other things. Because they are big and strong, a woman would not be able to stop them. They might even try to *steal one of us dogs*!

We hear a raucous, wall-shaking thud. They must be jumping on our roof! Horace looks out the window, but he doesn't see anything. Kate is out getting groceries. We go on full alert!

Through the window, we see Charles' car pull up to the yard. Charles runs around the car to help Kate with the grocery sack. We hear Mrs. M yell out, "Baboons!" Charles takes the sack from Kate and rushes with her to the door. As they scramble inside, he says, "Oh yeah, the baboons can cause big problems. Better *stay* inside—they might even attack women," Charles warns us, as he puts down the grocery sack. Kate thanks him, and he leaves.

A few minutes later, the landlords are at the door. Mr. M has a *shotgun* in his arms. I know it has an exploding noise, and the sight of it makes me shiver in fear. We both start barking and whining. Mom and Horace tell us to shush. I tell Romie, "I was afraid of guns since my days of running the streets with Rex. We experienced gunshots a couple of times."

He says, "I'd also come across them when a drunken guy shot one near the bushes where I hid in front of the bar."

Then the landlord says, "A whole troop of baboons could be on their way. If they're still here by morning time, I will kill the biggest one. That'll make them go away."

I think that is a horrible idea. I put my head down. I slink out of the room and end up sniffing around on the semi-enclosed back patio. I discover a gap in part of the ironwork. It looks like I could fit through. I peek outside and don't see anyone. I'm thinking that I'll just have a quick pee and come right back in. When I go out in the yard, I see the back of a small monkey who's sitting on the lawn by himself. It looks a lot like the one who jumped on me. He doesn't see me, so now I have my chance to teach him a lesson and give him back the scare he gave me.

I pounce on his head from behind. I growl fiercely. He's pretty small, so my fourteen pounds are enough to knock him over. After he starts screeching, I bite him on the back of the neck, and he doesn't fight back. When he goes down on his side, I can see he is *not* the same monkey that jumped on me before. His head is much wider, and his coat is thicker and heavier.

Out of nowhere, an enormous baboon comes running across the lawn towards us, screeching. I panic. *Oh no, I'm done for!* It's the small one's mother. She doesn't pay any attention to me. She snatches her baby and cuddles him to her chest, examines him to see if he's okay. Then she turns around and whisks him back with her from wherever she came from in the corner of the yard. I creep back into the house. My heart is pounding out of my chest, and I'm trembling all over.

No one knows I've been outside. I'm still catching my breath. When I return to the living room, I find the landlady and her husband still there. The husband is telling us that, once the baboons land, it's hard to get rid of them, and that, although it's against the law, he intends to scare them off that night with gunshots. "And if they don't go, one of them will pay the ultimate price," he says, as he waves his gun and snickers.

I'm worried. I don't know the baboons, but I saw that the mother baboon is a caring mom and protects her baby. Neither she nor the baby tried to fight with me. The whole idea that the landlord might shoot one of them makes me feel awful. I skulk into the bedroom.

I know Kate doesn't like their plan, either. From the back room, I hear her ask, "Is there any way they might go away by themselves?"

Mr. M tells her, "Only if they feel threatened by something. Shooting one is how we show our dominance over them. Otherwise, they'll make a home on our property."

Sometimes I wish I could speak English. I want to tell Mommie what happened with me and the baboons, even though, for sure, she would get upset.

Darkness comes. We can't sleep waiting to hear the thumping on the roof or the sound of a gun. But it doesn't come. Same with the next day and night. We're still nervous. After the third night, when the baboons still don't seem to be around, that's when I let Romie know what happened. Romeo tells me, "Maybe the baboons aren't coming back because of *you*. You frightened them away."

"*Really?* I never thought of that," I say. I suppose it's a possibility. Maybe the mother baboon thinks *I'm a danger* to her baby.

"Those baboons don't want someone like *you* messing with their little baby," Romie tells me. He licks my ear.

He makes me smile and I say, "After all, I *am* a warrior princess. *Heh heh!*"

The skies continue to be gray, and the sun only peeks out for short periods. It's still cold in the old house. Horace makes a fire in the fireplace. It only heats a small area. Kate is allergic to the smoke.

One day, Kate says we're going to move. She says we've had enough. We just aren't enjoying the lifestyle here or climate or the intruding landlords. Besides, she says, she can't find a way to work with elephants. The government doesn't want to give out any new work permits for working with elephants. And if we are to stay more than a few months, we have to get a work permit.

I think she means we are going home to California. That would be okay.

But no. She will take the job working at AfricaGirls in Diani

Beach. She'll teach the young mothers about elephants and monkeys and trees and how to take care of them. She has decided it will be a fun and worthwhile thing to do. And we could enjoy the beautiful beach and the warm air.

So Mom and Grandpa start gathering all our things together and preparing for our move. We are excited because we loved our time at the beach. The sun was shining, the beach was beautiful, and the monkeys were playful. We have never felt comfortable in this big, cold house. The botanical garden yard is nice, but we never know when an eagle might swoop down, a monkey would holler, or the neighbor dogs would give us attitude.

We're going to live in the Wayside Apartments! We'll be able to frolic on the beach every day. It sounds like a great plan. We do our happy dance! When we looked at that apartment a few months ago, we thought about what it would be like to live there. We liked the grand rooms, the large patios, and the gigantic yard.

Charles comes over to say goodbye. He tells us they still have the dog his son found on the street—the cute little white dog. Only now, he's not as small. The boy wants to keep him forever. Kate gets excited and encourages Charles to let his son keep the dog, whom they have named Snowy.

Kate reminds him, "Dogs can be great companions for kids. It will mean so much to him—to your family. You know, Roxie and Romeo—they are such an important part of *our* family." She winks at us.

Charles says, "Yes, I know, but we're not used to having dogs in the house, and it's quite a change for us. My wife isn't sure, either."

Kate says, "Try it. I can see you like Roxie and Romeo. This could be fun for you and your family. Call me if you want to talk about anything—I'd love to help. And let us know how it's going."

Chapter 8

ROMEO – More Elephants Please

We're finally packed and ready to go. I'm hoping that we'll stop at that wildlife lodge with the waterhole on the way back. Maybe we'll see the big elephant who gave us a drink and sang with us last time.

We finally get to the lodge. Roxie and I pull Kate on our leashes towards the patio dining room where we met the elephant. We run to the left where the waterhole is. We finally spot it, but there aren't any animals to see. Kate says we must be patient when looking for wild animals. We never know for sure when or where they will show up.

She says we'll have lots of time to see them. We'll have something to eat and take a walk, then we'll get settled in our room and we'll come back to the waterhole again later. We do all those things, but I keep looking around, imagining that an elephant may pop up out of the blue.

Still, we can't see any elephants. When we return to the patio later, we see an animal in the distance. Agile and fast, he comes galloping towards the waterhole and he spots us right away. He inches closer to the patio. Mom says he's a an impala. Another free-spirited animal who lives in the wild. He has large antlers. He is curious and brave, staying close and looking right in our eyes. Then he bends down and takes a drink of water before he runs off back toward the trees. It's thrilling to watch him.

***

After eating our dinner, we keep hanging around on the patio, on the lookout for more animals. Kate calls out, "Giraffes!" Oh wow. Tall, exotic creatures are munching on leaves way up high. They are on the side of the field. So pretty! Oh! And here come a group of zebras playing with each other on the other side. What a wonderland this is! We don't have anything like this in California! It's going to be hard to sleep tonight. It turns out our bedroom has a partial view where we can see some trees and the right corner of the field. I stay by the window all night long.

In the middle of the night, I hear a low growling sound. I stare out in the blackness until my eyes can pick up a few details. Suddenly, I see an animal running across the field, followed by two bigger animals. I think they are lions. I start howling. Kate wakes up. "What is it, Romie?" I keep staring out the window and howling. She tells me to shush.

She listens at the window, then she hears the growling sound too. She gets excited.

"Come on," she says. She grabs her flashlight and pulls on her jacket. She hooks me and Roxie up and we tiptoe out the door, down the long hallway towards the side where the patio and waterhole are. I yip. She tells me again, "Shush!"

We creep out to the patio. It's hard to see, but the longer we look, we can start to see a few little things. We walk along the outer bannister, listening for those exotic sounds. About midway across, we pick up the faint sounds of eating. We stop and stare into the night. She turns on the flashlight. Out midway in the field, there are a few lions in a kind of circle. They are all eating. We look and look. Suddenly, Kate says, "It's a baby giraffe!" She tears up. Roxie and I also feel stricken. Those beautiful giraffes we saw earlier—and now their baby is getting eaten. This is hard to absorb. We hang our heads. This is life in the wild.

Kate says, "Come on, let's go get some sleep." We go back to our room. Any fantasies I started to harbor about life in the wild are squashed. I don't know if I would have the stomach or the guts for it. I think the heaviness of the scene helps me to go to sleep. Sometimes sleep can be a comfort. Roxie and I both sleep close to Mom that night. We all hug and appreciate the comforts we bring each other.

***

The next morning, we get up and Mom packs up our things. We load up the car, then we go out to the patio. We see Horace and our driver, Colon, having coffee.

We slowly head towards the waterhole. What a surprise! What a scene! Dozens of elephants are visiting the field. There are a few reaching for fruit on a tree. There are big ones, medium-sized ones, and little babies! (Of course, they are a lot bigger that I am, but when standing next to the bigger ones, they look tiny, even to me!) So cute! Both the big ones and the medium-sized ones are hovering over the babies, as if to protect them. Sometimes they stand right underneath the big one. Kate tells us that is the mother, and the medium-sized ones are the babies' sisters. Kate says that elephants are very good caretakers of their young. Whenever there is a little baby,

the whole herd pitches in to keep her safe. The young female elephants all love to play "nanny" to the babies.

What a peaceful setting. Kate snaps lots of photos. We can hardly eat. We just want to get a good look at all these creatures. Kate says, "If a lion tries to eat the baby elephant, the big elephants will protect her. The lions know the elephants are big and strong, and they would not want to get kicked or trampled by them." We look around the field. So many elephants. One is scratching his back on a tree trunk. Another one is waiting for his turn. Roxie chuckles when she sees that. Kate says, "Aren't they wonderful! I just love all these elephants and how they live with and take care of their families!" And I completely agree. If I were an elephant, I would feel so safe and secure if I belonged in that family.

We linger as long as we can. But Colon tells us we should get back on the road. "There is some construction ahead, and we don't want to be driving in the dark."

Chapter 9

ROXIE – Monkeys in Our House

*W*hen we arrive at the Wayside Apartments, there is a team of helpers waiting for us. Jackie and Renson and Babu help us unpack the car and get things up to our penthouse apartment. They introduce themselves and look happy to see us—and we appreciate their help.

We climb three long flights to get upstairs, but we're used to stairs. They remind us of our own townhouse in California. I think, *Is that still our home? Are we ever going back?*

Jackie and Renson talk to us a lot. Other people work there, too, and as we pass them by, they are always smiling at us. In fact, they are constantly calling our names, even if they don't want us to come to them. At first it's confusing, since we were taught to come when called, but I finally realize they're not asking us to *come*, what they are doing is saying, "Hi!" Then we realize that, to them, calling our names means they *like* us, it makes us feel at home. They are a more relaxed group of people than the people in the city. They don't seem to worry about so many things. This makes us all relax more, too, even

Kate and Horace.

No sooner do we get our stuff up in the apartment than a monkey goes dashing by us in the living room! He steals a mango Mom had bought on the side of the road and then he jumps right out the third-floor window! Romie and I go berserk! How dare he! We jump up on the couch and bark our loudest warnings to the critter. Mom and Horace look out the window and see there's a big palm tree two feet away. This is the monkeys' ladder to heaven, as they can jump right in whenever they want and steal our food.

Horace says we must keep the window closed. But Kate says she will not live by the beach and stay closed up inside. We have to enjoy the perfect temperatures and not be prisoners in our own apartment. They argue. I can see both sides. Mom doesn't give up. She says maybe we can build a monkey fence over the window so it doesn't have to close. Finally, they decide to give it a try. Horace is skeptical and Mom is certain, as usual. I guess if she didn't feel so strongly about things, we wouldn't even be here. She makes all the plans and Grandpa goes along and enjoys the fruits of her labor, or else I guess he would pick up the pieces if something went wrong.

Romeo says, "But usually it turns very positive. Kate is the one who decided to adopt me—a wounded street urchin." Horace commits to a new venture once it has been decided. Then he embraces it as his own. Kind of the wind beneath our wings or something like that. Still, we don't like it when they argue. We want to tell them to "be more elephant!"

It becomes evident that monkeys are everywhere! These monkeys are definitely more playful than the ones we met in the city. We learn that the people who live at the beach are used to having wild animals around them and aren't afraid, even when they spot a baboon. The wild animals are much more used to people, too. That's why monkeys jump into our apartment window. Kate finds some workmen who will make a monkey fence for the window. After they install the fence, the monkeys jump on the fence, only to look disappointed they can't get in. Whenever we see them, we bark and shout at them from our side of the window. Their expressive faces are fun to watch. They desperately want to sneak in to see what we're doing and what we're eating.

They sometimes leap and swing onto our open patio and tiptoe inside through our patio door to steal something. Right from under our noses, one steals a grapefruit! (Another time, it's a bag of peanuts!) When they get into our house, we scream and chase them as hard as we can. We try to catch them, but it's more like a game. It feels like they are part of life when we chase them. After a while, we get used to their presence. When we see them outside on the grass, we don't try to go after them or bark at them—as long as they mind their own business!

***

We notice some new kinds of monkeys jumping in the trees. These have long, black hair with touches of white and long, white tails, and they're the biggest ones we have ever seen. Kate says they are called colobus, and they're very rare and endangered. I feel sad when she says that, at one time, people used to capture them in order to use their gorgeous long hair for

themselves. She likes them a lot. The colobus don't tease us, and they keep to themselves. But they are beautiful to look at. We can watch them at eye level when they're in the trees and we're on our patio—doggie television!

Kate meets Nancy and Luciana, two leaders of an organization that helps save the colobus and other monkeys. It's called Colobus Conservation. They save injured monkeys and rescue monkeys that people have tried to keep as pets. Being wild animals means they don't like to be with humans all the time like dogs do, and it's not good for them. They need to stay outside with their monkey families and hunt for food for themselves. The rescuers help the little monkeys—who were stolen from their monkey moms in order to become humans' pets—to get back with other monkeys and learn to be wild again.

Some members of Colobus Conservation weave long ladders that stretch from one side of the road to the other way up in the trees. This is for the monkeys to run high over the roadway to the opposite side without getting hit by a car. I enjoy meeting more hero people who help animals. They are the smart ones because their jobs show that they know all animals are important.

Kate and Horace buy a huge new television. They can't find all the channels like we had back at home, but they find out how to watch movies, especially old movies. Every evening they watch classic films while Romeo and I rest beside them. One of their favorites is called *Casablanca*. "Here's lookin' at you, kid!" We must have seen it a dozen times. I'm surprised Kate didn't try to name one of us after that movie. In that case, I would be Ilsa and Romeo would be Rick. *Heh heh!* (I'm glad they didn't do that.) I remember that in the movie the people were talking about Paris and how they will always have it. Then I doze off. There will be more to explore tomorrow.

Chapter 10

ROMEO – Beach Dogs

Soon, we head out for a walk on the beach with Mom. A group of fishermen hang out at the driveway that goes between our little road and the beach. They all say hello to Kate. She smiles. One of them follows along with us and attempts to engage with her. I can tell Mom is not sure if she wants to be friends with him. But she is cordial. I am on my guard. Lots of people on the beach are gaping at us.

Later, we learn that most of the dogs around here have to live outdoors or in cages all day, and they only walk around at night to guard the property. Some never get to leave their yard or eat anything but scraps. So we are sure to always stay near our parents, especially when there are crowds of people nearby or when they stare at us.

The sand is soft and smooth. It feels so good on my paws. We stay on the leash for a while, then Mom lets us run up the beach a ways. In California we live near a beach, too. But there, dogs are not allowed to run on the beach or even to walk on the beach. Sometimes a lifeguard would tell us we are not allowed.

But here in Kenya, it's free-wheeling. Like those times we

drove up the coast of California and stayed in little hotels along the way. That was lots of fun. This is kind of like that, except there, people accepted us as part of the landscape. Here, we can tell already, we are considered to be something different, something new to the everyday life on the beach. Kate tells us, "Some people may like you, but they may only use animals as a way to make money for themselves, not to love them as companions." She and Horace love us and treat us better than anyone else. That is an important difference.

Kate says that, unfortunately, people in all parts of the world take advantage of animals. Like at home, in the circus, where we protested for the rights of animals. She says, "Some people feel superior and don't think about the fact that *they* are animals, too. All animals are wonderful. Just like humans, all feel love and pain and have something to contribute." After learning all this, Roxie and I are both *more* cautious than ever and stick even closer to her. She calls us to her—and we go right away (most of the time, anyway).

Mommie keeps a watchful eye on us. She never lets us wander around anywhere alone, even on the grounds of our apartment building. We hear from a neighbor that there are dog thieves around, and that dogs were recently snatched from a nearby yard. *Oh no!* That would be so horrible to be *stolen* and never see Mommie and Grandpa again. What would those thieves do with us? I dare not think about it.

Soon people are walking over to us. They say to Kate, "Nice dogs."

She says, "Thank you."

Then they say, "Give me one."

Kate is startled. *"Haha!* No, these are *my* doggies."

They say, "Aw come on, you have two. Just give me one."

Mom tries to slither away from the small group. But they follow us. We walk faster and faster. Soon they are way behind.

I say to Roxie. *"Give* them one! Humph! At least in Nairobi they wanted to *buy* us. Here they want us for free."

Then the beachboy who was following us comes running over. "I just wanna say, it's better if you don't tell anyone their names—because one day, when you're not lookin', they call their names and the dogs might go."

Kate looks at him. "Yes, I suppose you are right about that."

Then he says, "Let's go up the beach and have a drink."

Kate says, "I have to get home now." He says, "Maybe some other time." She smiles and keeps walking fast. The guy has trouble keeping up with us. It makes me wonder if Kate will ever have another boyfriend. I know she was married, and Roxie says Gerard was a great dad and loved Kate a lot. Maybe she just hasn't found anyone else who's good enough. We don't mind having her to ourselves.

I look behind at the fisherman guy and see he's lagging way behind us. That's when I notice the people who live at the beach walk slower than other people we've met here, and they talk slower, too. I guess that's because they come from a different tribe. Kate tells us, "There are lots of different tribes of people in Kenya and they all have their own special customs and language." She chortles, "It's kind of like a tribe of Shepherds and a tribe of Bulldogs, and a tribe of terriers!" *Haha!* A tribe of terriers! I guess Roxie and I are some kind of terriers—a *know-it-all terriers tribe!* Roxie thinks that's funny, too. We both break out into our wiggling and laughing duet. Kate chuckles, too, as we walk back to our new apartment. It's great when a mom has the same sense of humor as her pets!

There waiting for us is Amigo, who also lives at Wayside. He's a different kind of dog. People call him a Kenya beach dog. He's three times as big as us, but he likes us and wants our attention. Roxie likes him right away, and, as usual, in the beginning, I am aloof. I have to check things out before I give my friendship so freely. Especially since he's from a different tribe. *Haha.*

***

The next day, Mom has a meeting at the girls' village. We want to go with her, but she doesn't know if the students will have their babies with them. Kate explains to us, "The babies will all probably chase after you if you go, and you know you won't like that too much. They might try to pull your hair." She calls for a taxi and we are a little sad. She's our ringmaster of fun. Horace is checking something on his computer.

Roxie and I lull around the place, checking out all the rooms. When we go out on the patio, we see monkeys in the trees. A colobus monkey family is sitting close to each other, munching on flowers. We watch them for a while. When they jump from one tree to the next, the whole tree shakes. Roxie and I snicker at each other. Not too graceful. Mostly they just hang out and eat. From our patio, we can see all the people at the building working and scuttling around below.

There's the large swimming pool. Renson has a pole with a net on the end and he runs it through the water, picking up leaves which have fallen in. Babu is sweeping the sidewalks with a small broom and watering the plants. Jackie is talking on the phone and supervising. They seem like a friendly crew. And there's Amigo lying in the grass.

There's a beep. A car is outside the gate. Babu runs over to the gate and opens it for the car. While he's doing that, we see Amigo sneaking to the side. After the car comes inside, he quickly dashes around the car and out the gate. Babu yells, "Amigo!" but he's too late. Amigo is out of there. We don't know whose dog Amigo is. They might get upset when they find out he ran away.

Later, when Kate comes back, she takes us outside to walk to the beach. Surprisingly, Amigo is back inside the grounds.

He comes to greet us and wants to go out the gate when we leave. Mom calls Jackie and asks if he's allowed to come out. She says he's not supposed to go, but he sneaks down to the beach all the time. She says, if we want to, she'll find his leash and we can take him with us. Mom says we can try it tomorrow. Jackie yells at Amigo to stay inside. She picks up a rock and acts like she will throw it at him. He backs away, back into the yard.

We have to go down the same driveway we went through yesterday to get to the beach. We see it's still crowded. The same group of guys, who I guess are fishermen, are sitting there. They all call out to Kate. "Hey mama, how are you? Going for a walk on the beach?" Some whistle. "Do ya want some company?" Mom smiles at them as she picks up the pace. I can tell they make her nervous. I'm glad we're there to protect her. If someone tried to mess with her, I would growl and bite. I hope it doesn't come to that, though.

The beach is splendid, as it was yesterday. We walk far up the sand, and where there are few people, we are allowed to run off leash and explore. Roxie and Mom like to walk with their feet in the water. I like to run the other way, to the inner edge of the beach where different landscapes begin off of the sand.

Mom and I are always on the lookout for our safety. Most people are plenty laid-back. I worry about some of the men, as I catch a lot of them eyeing Mom with interest. Protecting her is my number one job. And I know she is on the lookout for possible dognappers. We are her "babies" and she has a strong, canine-like instinct to protect us.

Later in the evening, we go back to the apartment and we get some supper. Mom and Grandpa decide to explore a restaurant down the road.

As we are leaving the complex, Amigo comes over. Mom pets him and Roxie rubs against him. He comes to greet me too, and we bump noses. As we are going out the gate, he follows us. Kate can't convince him to go back inside. Hesbon, the gatekeeper, says, "Just let him go with you, it'll be okay." Then we walk up the main road to catch a ride. Amigo follows us. There are cars on the road as well as tuk-tuks. This turns out to be a problem, because we can't bring Amigo with us. Yet it is dangerous on the road. Vehicles are whizzing by. As we wait for a ride, Amigo walks up ahead. We see him crisscrossing in front of the traffic. Mom calls to him, but he doesn't pay attention. She gets worried. Suppose he gets run over? She calls to him some more, but he just keeps on going. He dodges the cars, but suppose one comes too fast? Horace says there's nothing we can do. A tuk-tuk stops and asks if we want a ride. We pile in.

Tuk-tuks are little open-air vehicles. Fun to ride in. Roxie didn't like them at first because, with their small wheels on dirt roads, they can be very bumpy. I see that she adjusts by sitting with her nose pointed out to catch as much fresh air as possible. Kate is still thinking about Amigo and so am I. We would feel awful if something happened to him. Horace says, "He must have done this before with other people. He is smart and knows his way around." This might be true. I hope he doesn't try to follow our tuk-tuk.

We go down the road a few miles and, after about ten minutes, turn into another small road on the beach side. This road has what looks like a dense jungle on both sides. Very thick foliage and trees. I bet the monkeys like it here! At the end of the road, we get out and there is a restaurant called Nomads with lots of patios looking out over the ocean. We all like it here and I can't wait to explore the beach and see if it's the same as ours. While Horace orders a drink, Kate walks us out to the beach. We saunter up the shoreline. Almost no one is on the beach. She lets us run free. We run and run and then we come back to match her pace. We always come back. Why wouldn't a dog come back if they have a loving human to come back to? We all run together a bit, enjoying the breezes, and it's great fun. Mom walks us down by the waves. It's starting to get dark, but there are lights pointing towards the surf.

We come back up to the patio so Kate and Horace can eat their dinner. They were thoughtful enough to bring us our dog beds so we can sit comfortably under the table. Nomads becomes one of our favorite outings. Sometimes we get to taste the food from Mom's plate. Yes, we think we're going to like it here, spoiled and privileged as can be. We are starting to realize this is what people may think when they look at us accompanying Kate everywhere. Most of them probably couldn't imagine our rough beginnings.

At home in California, we could see other dogs around us enjoying the good life with families, nice homes and new collars, going on walks, hikes, and excursions like we did. While we didn't stand out at home, we always felt that we were some of the most loved dogs on our block. But when we see dogs in Africa, the differences are immense. It's hard for us to imagine living their lives. I don't know if I would have the courage to be one of them. Even though my life started badly and I was barely surviving, I have become used to my comforts and privileges and would never want to go back. It dawned on me that what we have is so *very special.*

After dinner, we all get in a taxi that is waiting at the entrance to the restaurant, and the driver takes us safely back to our new home. It's pretty dark, with no lights along the road. And there are no lights on our little street where we live. When we pull up to the gate, the night watchman opens it for us, and we go in. We look for Amigo but he's not there. We get lumps of worry in our throats. The next day he is sitting on the lawn when we go outside as though everything is normal.

Roxie adds, "We can see that Amigo is lonesome. It's a shame he doesn't have a mom or dad. Kate likes him a lot, and the longer we stay here, the friendlier we all get. He runs after her and she pets him and plays with him. We all go to the beach together. When Mom occasionally lets us off leash, we run around with Amigo. When we don't see him, we worry that something might have happened to him. Often, he comes over to me and Romie and gives us kisses. I love Amigo so much. I wish he lived with us all the time."

***

I admire Amigo, too. But, in a way, he is too wild. Outside the gate of our apartment building, there are some people and dogs he doesn't like. He gets angry and barks at them ferociously. When he doesn't like a person, he barks at them until they turn blue in the face or until they get intimidated and angry. When that happens, they usually threaten him with stones. Some even hit him with a stick.

Some days, when we pass by a tourist lodge on the corner,

there are two guard dogs who growl and look mean. Mom says they are Rottweilers. When they see us, they act like they want to kill us all—especially Amigo, who looks for them every day. If he sees them, he growls first and snarls to remind them he is in charge. Amigo doesn't like the Rotties, and they all start barking furiously at teach other. Mom calls for Amigo to come, but he would rather stay and act mean. Usually the Rotties are on chains.

But one day, a Rottweiler is loose. He and Amigo have a loud screaming match and start attacking each other. *Oh no!* There goes Amigo who will never back down. Before we know it the other Rottie joins in and they are both attacking our friend Amigo. Mom screams at the top of her lungs, "Come get your dog!" We are on leash and stay close to Mom but we are both terrified. Suppose the Rotties come after us? Kate keeps screaming, "Come get your dogs right now! There's a fight!"

Finally, a guy comes out and pulls the Rotties off of Amigo. Amigo is wounded. Mom slips his leash on him and we head back to the Wayside Apartments. Poor Amigo is bleeding and torn all over. Mom tells Jackie and Renson, "We must take him to a vet."

Jackie calls the building owner and he says he will pay us back if we take him to a vet. Kate insists Renson come with us, and we all end up walking about a half mile down the side of the road to see Dr. Paul. Kate tells Dr. Paul the story. Dr. Paul knows those guard dogs. He says there used to be three, and one of them died from *rabies*. The manager of the building refused to get the others vaccinated. "Now," he says, "it is possible one or both of them might have rabies, too." Doctor Paul tells Kate that many dogs are never vaccinated by their owners. And there are many stray dogs, too, that nobody vaccinates. There's no shelter for them, either.

I didn't know it before, but it turns out Roxie and I both have shots against rabies. So does Amigo. But lots of dogs here do not have vaccinations. It makes them dangerous. If a dog with rabies bites you or even scratches you, you can die. Dr. Paul gives Amigo two shots in the leg—one for rabies and one with antibiotics.

I think about how a couple of times, when we were walking on leash, stray dogs wanted to come over to us. We would like to say hello. Now we've learned to be on our guard. In fact, we'll never be able to make friends with any of those poor stray dogs. I don't think I had shots before I was rescued, either. Luckily, I never had rabies. But it's different in California from Africa, where rabies is more widespread.

Not only can those dogs give us rabies, but also they are mean and they could easily chew us up or kill us. We are much smaller dogs. Mom says she doesn't feel safe having them on the corner. Every time we go to the beach, we have to pass by them. And usually no one is watching them. When we get back to the Wayside Apartments, she calls the owner. She says, "Can you please do something and help get that neighbor's guard dogs vaccinated and tied down when we go by?" She tells him about Amigo and the vet. She tells him, "We don't feel safe living here with those unvaccinated dogs running wild. They are a danger and a menace to people as well as dogs. Our dogs are especially in danger since they're small. If you can't help us take care of the situation, for our own safety, we will have to move."

Kate says the landlord told her he knows the owner of the lodge and will call and talk to him.

The next day, Kate calls the KSPCA (Kenya Society for the Protection & Care of Animals) and asks for help. They don't have a branch in our town and rarely come down there, they told her. They know it's a problem and there are lots of stray dogs there without vaccines. This means we will have to be extra careful and not make friends with any other dogs. Not only do dogs have to live outside and act mean and eat only scraps, but they could also get a deadly disease and die.

Meanwhile, Amigo gets lots of extra attention from the staff. Renson gives him a bath, and we go and visit him as he mopes around. He doesn't have a mom or dad. Yes, he has friends at the Wayside Apartments and I think some of them like him a lot. Others think he's a pain in the butt—especially since Mom has been talking to the owner and he has warned the staff not to let Amigo sneak out. It means extra work for them to look after Amigo.

In other ways, I look up to Amigo. He is so independent. He knows who his friends are— and who his friends are not.

But he hasn't learned to keep his feelings to himself at all. He goes on walks with us, and everywhere we go, he has friends who call to him and enemies whom he tries to attack. It's all Kate can do to keep him calm sometimes. But I do know he loves us. He greets us and kisses us every day. And he is crazy about Kate. When he sees her, he gets so excited he jumps up on her, but then he ends up scratching her arms. It's warm around here so she often has her arms exposed. They are full of pink scratch marks.

Finally, Kate convinces Jackie and Renson to go on walks with us a few times a week so they can help control Amigo. We feel safe with him there because we know he would protect us. If a dognapper tried to grab one of us, Amigo would tear off his arm.

**

Occasionally, Horace goes on a walk with us. Once I hear Kate tell her father, "The people who live near here are sweet and laid-back. But they are not well educated about nature and wildlife. And look at how many young girls have babies. Since I started working at AfricaGirls, I have noticed many more girls on the street with babies. Hari says once they have a baby, they never go back to school.

"Wouldn't it be great to start a school just for young girls and women and their babies? We could foster new leaders in the community who are in tune with nature. We could call it the Elephant Matriarch School.

"We could center all their academic subjects on nature. When they are learning math, they could study the sizes of elephant herds. When they learn geography, they can learn about the vastly different areas of their country and its topography—what animals live there, for example. I have discovered in my short time at AfricaGirls that, even though these girls are surrounded by monkeys, not one of them could tell me the names of the different types of monkeys! This would be a great project, and maybe one day I will try to put it together. I think Hari might help, too! If these girls could get a good education, they could teach their neighbors to respect elephants and other animals. You know the old saying, 'The hand that rocks the cradle rules the world.'"

Horace says, "It's a great idea. I'm proud to have raised such a smart and caring girl as you. I'm sure you have the smarts and persistence to make it happen."

A few days later, the Rottweilers are gone. I now realize it is due to the persistence of Kate.

Kate muses, "I wonder where they went. Why didn't the owners get them their rabies shots? How come nobody is helping the poor stray dogs? Why isn't there any dog shelter?" Now I understand what dog shelters are for. It was tough for me being in one, but I see how stray dogs need care. Most of them are skinny and look sad. I wonder if that's how I looked when I was a stray puppy. We never find out what happened to the Rotties. At least we won't feel like we're going to have a heart attack whenever we see one. Thank goodness I wasn't a stray dog in Africa. I may not even be *alive* anymore. I put my head down and rest.

I remember when I was a puppy on the street. I would get frightened a lot. I felt horrible that no one wanted me. I didn't know about all the dangerous things that could happen. I had no one to help me, and there was so little I understood. I hope Mom will be able to help the girls and their babies, too. Then maybe they can all help save the elephants and the dogs.

Chapter 11

ROXIE – I'm a Lovely Lady

When Mom is talking with the KSPCA on the phone, they tell her there will be an event coming up for dogs. A little dog show in town. The proceeds will go to benefit stray dogs and dogs who need vaccination and shelter. I hear her voice perk up. "Oh, that sounds great. We will definitely join in and bring our Roxie and Romeo!" Mom tells us all about it when she gets off the phone.

We don't know what to expect but we know we are going to some type of outing soon. She gives us each a bath. It's a kind of half-bath and half-shower (in the shower, with plastic tubs that people here use for washing clothes. We don't have a bathtub.) By the time we are finished, Mommie is all wet, too, and so is the floor. For a final touch, she brushes our teeth, and she brushes my now long and ungroomed hair.

The dog show is at a country club at the other end of town, so we hail a tuk-tuk to take us there. Kate says it is put on by *expats*—who are mostly older people from different countries who choose to make Kenya their home. Some of them have brought their dogs with them or adopted African dogs. Picnic tables are strewn around a field. I feel shy and stick close to

Mom. Romie does too.

At the dog show, there are different categories, just like the ones we see on television dog shows in the US. It seems funny to have one out here in the open. The ones on TV are so regulated and timed. While we are waiting, two big dogs get into a fight! We know we're not in Westminster now! The dogs are huge, as are most of the dogs at the show. Luckily their people get them under control. I think, "Good thing Amigo isn't here!"

Kate buys tickets to enter the different contests. People are coming up to me and telling Kate how *adorable* I am that day. Romie says, "You are definitely the prettiest one here." I smile and kiss Romie's nose. Romeo says, "Mom says there's a competition coming up for 'Loveliest Lady.' She thinks maybe you can win, and *I think so too!*"

There's another competition for "Best Rescue Dog" and she buys tickets for both of us. Romeo says "I feel so nervous, I'm afraid I'll start hopping on three legs. I try to calm myself down."

We are sitting outside at a picnic table as the other dogs and their guardians are. We hear the announcer call out the contest for "Loveliest Lady." Mom grabs my leash and we head for the center area. People are walking their dogs around in a circle. Romie stays on the side with Horace. Romeo says, "I think to myself—she's my girl! And Kate! My other girl! They are stars! I am one lucky dog."

And there are all different sizes and types of dogs. They call out *two* Roxie's. There's a Roxy with a *y* and a Roxie with an *ie*. We walk around a few times and Kate has to answer some questions.

It is fun! Suddenly they are calling out third place winner, a dog named Mitzy—one of the only tiny dogs at the fair. She is so old and tiny she can barely walk. Second prize is a dog named Brownie. She's a pretty big lab.

When it comes to first place, my heart is thumping. We hear, "It's Roxie with an *ie*!" We did it! We won the prize! Cameras are flashing! Mom lifts me in the air and gives me a big kiss. The judges come over and give me a red ribbon to wear! Mom's happy! Romie's happy! Horace is happy! I wear my award ribbon proudly. I already knew I was a *warrior princess*, but now I am a *lovely lady*, too! *Heh heh!* What a great day! Kate and I go to the center and have our picture taken. They present us with a huge bag of dog kibble. It's almost as big as Mom!

Then they continue to the next contest, which I didn't hear too well. But the one after that is "Best Rescue Dog." Mom takes Romeo and me out to the center ring. I prance around. Romeo seems to feel bashful with all eyes on him. Mom answers some questions about us and we walk around the circle a few times.

Romeo says, "I would be even more self-conscious if Roxie hadn't already rocked the house and was having such a good time. I try to look proud like she does, but I am worried about my leg. Sometimes it flares up and I don't want to look stupid. They can probably tell I have a slight limp, even when I try really hard."

The judging time starts. First, they call third place, and we hear "It's Roxie with an *ie*". Wow! I've won another award! I'm thinking, "They must really like me here!" Mom says we have to pay attention when they call second and first place, because we might hear Romeo's name—but no such luck. Rocko, one of the dogs who got into a fight, wins second prize, and a huge Great Dane named Giraffe wins top prize. We walk to the side. They give Kate the green ribbon for third prize.

Mom pins it on *Romeo* instead of me. "Now everyone has a prize," she says. Mom picks us both up for a hug and kisses. Horace takes our photo.

Romeo says, *"I know I didn't really win.* They are making

sure I don't feel bad. I play along. I didn't expect to win. I'm not a show dog. I'm more of an introvert. It's really not my thing."

I chime in: "Aah, poor BooBoo! You'll always be *our* first prize!"

Mom says there's a beautiful African saying, "How can one win unless we all win!"

Romeo says, "I am lucky my family loves me so much that they try to spare my feelings. Roxie loves me and is willing to share her good fortune."

"And the prize is..." more dog kibble! We smile and thank everyone. We don't usually eat kibble. Only once in a while for a quick change of pace. We decide we'll keep some of it for a treat, but we will give most of it to Amigo. He wasn't there today, but he is kind of skinny and maybe it will be good for him. We can't wait to get back and give him his present! It feels good to share. I understand why Kate gave Romeo the green ribbon. "It is better to give than to receive!"

Chapter 12

ROMEO – Neighborhood Animals

Almost every day, we walk down the side of the road with Kate.

Often, we walk to Kokko's Coffee Shop, where we like to sit on the patio while Mommie drinks a soy latte. One day, we come across a herd of cattle hanging out on the side of the road. Some are standing and others are reclining in the grass under trees. Roxie and I and the cows all pull our noses closer to get a better sniff. Some move away as we pass by. They are gentle and peaceful, and they don't use their bigger size to frighten us. We don't feel anxious—at least, not while we are with Kate. Besides the elephant, they seem like the most peaceful animals we have ever met.

We never saw cows back home. I wonder if they're somebody's pets. Kate says in the United States, cows live on farms. She says, "Some of them live in horrible 'factory farms,' where they can't even walk around. They have to stand in one place all day long."

I can feel how sweet and calm these cows are—and that

they aren't bothering anyone. Mom says a lot of people *eat* them. I'm glad my Kate and Horace are vegan. They never eat anything from animals. They never give us any cow meat to eat. I think, when we go back to California, we should go to one of those protests for animals and try to protect cows.

Every day we see monkeys and sometimes we see baboons. We don't go up to them and they don't confront us, either. They mind their own business. I think about how the people in Nairobi were so scared of them. Here, even though some people say they can be troublemakers, they are part of the village.

Sometimes we see the camels on the beach. Mom says people keep them to give rides to tourists. Since there aren't many tourists, the camels are mostly just walking up the beach and hanging out in the sand. They all seem very placid. Like that one, Obama, who licked Roxie.

One time, when we all go to visit Roselyn's house, she has lots of chickens in her yard. At first, we want to chase them, but Mom keeps us on leash. So we watch them from across the yard. They are hilarious. The way they strut around and peck things up off the ground. I wouldn't mind getting to know them better.

Another time, we see goats by the road. We pass them gingerly, as their movements are quick and nervous. After observing them two or three times, we know that they will not bother us. We walk in confidence. Sometimes the goats stare at us, and when we come near them, they *baa* and *maa* at us loudly and run away. Imagine! They see us two little dogs, and some of them are actually afraid of us. Even though they probably never saw any small dogs like us before, they accept us as fellow creatures. There are so many different kinds of animals.

Almost every animal we meet is wonderful and interesting and not dangerous. It's like a huge brotherhood and sisterhood. I feel happier and happier that I am part of it.

Chapter 13

ROXIE – Lessons at the Beach

Every day the beach is different. Sometimes, the ocean is still and far away. Other times, it's wavy and coming in. Kate says that's the tide at work—sometimes pulling the water outward, other times letting it roll back to shore. Some days there are little pools of water, and other days there are soft leaves from the sea all around us. I love to walk through the leaves and roll in them. Mom says it's like a spa treatment. I adore hopping around on the coral on the beach, getting my legs wet, chasing Romeo and getting chased.

Mom decides we should know how to swim. She lifts me up and walks out from the sandy beach, carrying me into the surf. When the water is up to her knees, she knows it's just above my head. She sets me down in the water, knowing the only way I can get back to shore is to paddle. It's unnerving not to feel the sand beneath my paws. I lose my pace and feel I am slipping in the water. She lifts me under my legs and gets me above sea level. I start again and get better and better at paddling. I have an innate ability to swim. Whereas at first I am skeptical, after we practice a few times, I feel more confident. Mom cheers me on. I look forward to our swimming lessons.

Romeo does not take to the water as quickly as I do, and when it's time for a lesson, he runs away from the shoreline. Mom thinks swimming would be helpful for his leg, but she doesn't take him in as much as she does me. She doesn't want to stress him out.

We don't get to be off leash much, especially not when there are lots of people around. Or when we see any other dogs nearby. No, that privilege is only for when the beach is mostly empty. It's because people still keep coming up to Kate and saying, "Give me one." People repeat that every day. They want her to give them one of *us*! Just like in the city where they wanted to buy me and Romie. Here they want us for *free*! *Humph!* People say, "They are beautiful," or, "They are nice dogs." Then they start in with the "Give me one" routine. That's when we walk away.

I guess a lot of people have never seen small dogs, and they think we're unusual. I don't see any designer dogs around. They may not have many here. Maybe they think that *we* are designer breeds! Even though a lot of people around here don't seem to be very rich, some people ask how much we cost. *Heh heh! Go away! We're priceless!*

***

Kate is getting more and more involved with her job. Many afternoons, she leaves us and goes off to work in a taxi, and it picks her up at the AfricaGirls center, too. She is given the title Environmental Director of AfricaGirls. She goes to see her girls every week and plans lessons and outings for them. She's teaching them about animals and taking care of nature. She wants them to learn the value of the trees and to protect dogs and all animals—especially elephants.

Kate's girls have little babies to take care of and haven't been able to experience the excitement of being young girls. Kind of like mama dogs who live in puppy mills, I've heard. They never have any fun or go anywhere. Nobody has ever taught them to appreciate all the beautiful nature around them, like the ocean and the trees and the animals. So, Kate takes them on little excursions. Sometimes they might go visit Colobus Conservation or do a beach cleanup or visit the Marine Center near Nomads. They are learning about the wonderful environment they live in and how to take care of it. Kate says the girls love their outings, and they're excited by all they are learning.

According to Mom, the girls in her classes have never seen a wild elephant, even though they live in the same country. They don't realize how wonderful elephants are and how important it is to protect them. Mommie says she wants them to be more "elephant"—just like us—learning to enjoy and take care of the earth.

Kate practices her lessons by telling us all the things she will teach. She teaches the girls that, "Elephants are in harmony with nature, and the earth depends on them to scatter seeds that make trees and plants grow. This provides more good living areas, called habitats, for all the other animals. When the forests grow from their seeds, it helps humans, too, and all living beings. The trees are the best answer we have for fighting climate change. We need the elephants to help save the earth from severe climate changes." She says that when there's no rain, and the earth gets too dry, elephants dig up water for their families and herds, and for other kinds of animals, too.

Mom makes copies of nature films to show the girls, since some of them do not speak a lot of English and it's harder for them to understand her. They must be very smart, though, since they all speak Kiswahili, the country language, and then they all speak the languages of their different tribes. English is their third language. We enjoy many cozy afternoons in front of the big screen TV watching animal films with her. We see videos of elephants living in big herds and see them digging up water from underground with their big tusks. Elephants know where to go to find good food. Their memories of the routes they used to take when they were babies helps them get where they need to go. They listen to the mama elephant, the matriarch. I think about the big elephant we met at the waterhole. When we were thirsty, he gave us water too! And he sang with us when we started to howl.

Romie says, "I am trying to understand these wild animals we are meeting. They *don't want to live with humans* and they depend on *each other* instead. Even the monkeys all stick together and share things. And help each other. They are very clever and very independent. I want to be more independent, too. You and I are part of a proud animal kingdom. I want to absorb this and feel it in my bones. Maybe one of these days some of their courage will rub off on me. I am so glad we got to meet all those beautiful elephants, and I hope we can meet more. I hope the girls can meet them, too."

Kate says, "Before we leave Africa, I'll find a way to take the girls to meet wild elephants—and that will be a very special day."

Chapter 14

ROMEO – Almost
Mr. Dogtober

One day, the sidewalk burns our paws. Even the dirt and the sand hurt them. The sun stings our eyes. We hang out in our air-conditioned bedroom. These days we stay in there all the time. We don't want to go out. We can hardly breathe. The day is hot. The night is hot. The air hot. It's the season of hot. Africa hot.

All the heat makes Mommie and us feel uncomfortable and in a bad mood. It goes on every day, day after day after day. She stays mostly in the room except when she goes to see her students. Horace doesn't mind the heat as much. He sits at his desk with the fan blowing on him. He's a quiet guy and keeps all his energy for himself most of the time. Maybe he can conserve his inner coolness better than the rest of us. The fall season usually cools things off in California, but here in Africa things happen at a different time of year. As the fall moves forward, it keeps getting hotter at the beach. Some of the schools are closed because it's too hot.

Around five o'clock, when it cools a little, there's some

shade on the beach. Then Kate takes us to the shore. It's the only time of day when the beach is shady. The water feels really great on our paws. It's the best part of the day, and we love to walk and run on the sand with Kate. Sometimes Roselyn comes, and sometimes Amigo does, too, with Jackie or Renson.

Kate says, "I need to go to Nairobi for an important meeting. I have to research some requirements about school licenses and credentials. If we are going to create a school, we need to know all the ins and outs. I have friends there who will share information with me. I might meet with someone from the government, too. Why don't we *all* go back to Nairobi for a break. It won't be as hot there like it is at the beach. We won't go back to our old home but stay in a little cottage nearby."

Kate and Horace agree and they are packing for the trip. We find a driver named Albert with a car and hunker down for the long, slow ride. Albert tells us that with Christmastime coming up in several weeks, the policemen want extra cash, and we have to be careful. At first, we don't understand why he is telling us this.

After about six hours of riding, we feel the car stop abruptly. A tall, round policeman standing on the road signals for Albert to come over. He gets out of the car and argues with the policeman. The policeman tells him he was speeding, so we all have to go to the police station.

Oh, no! We don't want to go.

Then the policeman opens the back door of our car! He pushes the dog bed out of the way and sits down next to Horace. We're surprised and—there's a look of surprise on his face, too. "What have we here?" the policeman asks, as if he doesn't know.

Kate and Horace stare at each other in fear and disbelief.

"Transporting animals? Let me see their papers."

Kate scrambles. "Papers? W-what papers?"

"Vaccination papers!"

"I didn't know we needed to carry them with us. We're not leaving the country."

"Yes! Whenever you transport animals, you need papers."

Kate has a bright idea. "Officer, they have their license tags on their collars from the United States. They were issued the end of last year, so they're still valid. You know, the government won't give them a license if they're not vaccinated."

She unclicks our collars from our necks and hands them to this man. He examines them, then says, "I need to see the yellow booklet with your veterinarian stamps."

"We have that, but it's at home where we live at the beach," she says.

The policeman replies, "Okay, I'll take the dogs to the police station, and you go back and get the papers."

Roxie and I look at each other, both of us feeling scared.

Kate pulls some African money out of her purse and hands it to him.

He says, "Ha! No! It will cost you five hundred dollars for all this. Let's get going."

Kate pleads, "No, please, these are my babies. I can't leave them."

She tries to hand him some more money. He still refuses and says we have to get going to the police station. I jump up into the front seat into Mom's arms and lick her face. Roxie holds her ground next to Horace in the back. I would've growled at the policeman, but I know that would make Mommie upset.

Kate starts to cry. "No, no! I can't live without my babies!" She reaches into her purse again and gives him what I guess is a lot of money—all that she has.

He examines it and a quick smile flashes across his face. "Okay, I'll let you go this time—but only because of Mama," he says as he waves his finger emphatically to the driver.

Kate is so upset—and then relieved once he leaves the car. This is a nightmare. There are so many policemen on the road—suppose it happens again? We don't have any more money. Will we all have to go to jail? She says if we go to the police station, who knows what may happen to us. I feel helpless because I wasn't able to protect Mommie from the mean man.

We keep going on our long drive, and eventually we relax again. *Not* a happy start to a vacation. And we don't even have time to stop at the waterhole lodge. We finally get to the city. It isn't nearly as hot as it is at the beach. We stay in a cabin that's part of a hotel where Kate has stayed before. The people who work there remember her and they are very friendly. Luckily, we don't have to see our old landlords and their crazy dogs. Val comes to dog-sit us at our cabin when Mommie and Grandpa go out to a movie. In between her business meetings, Kate calls a few friends and puts an itinerary together for us to explore nice parks and places in Nairobi.

***

Kate is reading a local newspaper and exclaims, "Oh, look at this! There's a big festival tomorrow. It's at a new mall not too far from here. Says they are having games for the kids and a *dog show*!" She turns to us, "What do you think, my little star babies? Do you want to go see the dog show? Maybe win some more prizes?"

It was surprising that we would find another dog show when it seemed like most people didn't do fun things with their dogs. But maybe some do! Kate says, "Let's call Charles, our old friend, to see if he's free to take us. I wonder how his family is doing with their son's dog, Snowy." Soon she is calling Charles and schmoozing on the phone. "Oh, really!

That's wonderful. How is Snowy? I love that name! You couldn't guess it's the name of an African dog! Aah! You'll tell us all about him when we see you."

We're glad to see him again. Charles happens to be just up the street, so he stops in to say hello in person. He pulls out some photos of his son and the dog. He says, "The whole family is now in love with Snowy." Charles tells us he took his wife and kids back to his ancestral tribal village recently for a family gathering, and they brought Snowy with them. He says the whole village thought he was nuts bringing a dog all that way in the car. After being there two weeks, slowly but surely, everyone in the village fell in love with Snowy. "In fact, some of my relatives are now planning to get themselves nice 'indoor' dogs, too."

After Charles leaves, Kate tells us that, here in Africa, we are helping to change people's attitudes about dogs. "See what you started? You are heroes. You are helping the dogs in Kenya. If more people see dogs behaving well and enjoying the outdoors with their people, more and more will do so. I am so proud of you!" And with her arms out, she encircles us both and gives us lots of kisses.

Wow, we both feel good about that—and kind of proud.

"So tomorrow we'll go to the festival and show them how beautiful you are. I bet lots of people will take photos of you two!" Mom smiles.

The next morning, we get our baths, teeth brushed, hair brushed and feel sparkling clean. Since we had already been in one show, it didn't seem as intimidating or new. I decided to just go and have fun and who cares if I win a ribbon? I'll be happy for Roxie if she wins. My little beauty.

It rained at night and it's muddy outside. We hop into Charles' car. Charles has an appointment so he says he will drop us off and pick us up later. We walk around the big, muddy grounds that are next to a new shopping center.

This is a bigger show than the last one we went to. Booths encircle the field and they are promoting different kinds of dog food. There are people with megaphones. They announce different competitions.

First, there's a competition for girl dogs. Mom walks Roxie around proudly. She is the smallest dog there. After a few minutes, I hear the mumbling sound on the megaphone. And names are being called. Roxie's name doesn't get called at all. Not for anything. I feel bad for her. But she says she doesn't care. She doesn't like the mud and is ready to come back to the sidelines. Kate is surprised they didn't pick her. "You are definitely the prettiest one," she says, as she gives her a big hug.

Next, the announcer says they are going to pick the star for the whole festival, Mr. Dogtober. He will be representing a dog food company. I don't really care. I'm just enjoying the fresh air and am glad to have a mom who likes to show us off! Most of the dogs are really big—bigger than I've ever seen. I like looking at them. There are lots of people with cameras too. I'm more at ease this time as we walk around the circle.

They call first runner-up. He is a huge brown dog. There's music and fanfare as they have him get up on a small podium and show off. Next, they say it's the runner-up. They make a big deal out of how hard it was to pick with so many great dogs. They call out, "Runner-up," then I hear my name, "Romeo! Will Romeo please come up to the stand?" We look around and no other Romeos are moving.

Mom looks at me and we are both surprised and gleeful. We prance around the ring again with many photographers snapping and clicking cameras. I get up on the podium like a star. People are asking what kind of breed I am! Kate says proudly, "He's a terrier mix—rescue dog!" I hear many people say how *handsome* I am! It's a little overwhelming! I was a wallflower. Now all of a sudden, everybody likes me! Roxie comes over to give me kisses.

I watch as they call Bruno, the name of the huge black dog, the biggest dog there. They say he was the champion last year, and he was so popular that they just had to pick him again. But they let me know that they sure like me, too. Admired by so many people, and my family so proud of me—it makes me tingle all over. I wouldn't have thought that I would feel strongly one way or the other, but I have to admit, winning is fun! All the adulation I receive feels like a warm shower on my ego. Maybe I'm shallow, but maybe everyone needs to have a little recognition once in a while, no?

***

The prize, as usual, is a big bag of dog food. Really big. Too big to try to bring it back to the beach with us. It turns out, there's a KSPCA animal shelter in the city. Maybe they would be able to accept the food. Kate calls them. Later that afternoon, we have Charles drive us over there. The shelter workers are very grateful to get the dog food.

A small group of homeless dogs at the shelter bark at us. I look at them and think about my days in the shelter. I sure have come a long way. From almost euthanized to almost Mr. Dogtober! Those dogs look at me mournfully. I know just how they feel.

Here I am, with a great family and sweet dog girlfriend. And a hero of the day, winning a prize from so many strangers. There they are, at the mercy of strangers and living in a cage. It's a far journey from where I had come—where these dogs are. I get a tear in my eye and send them good wishes with my mind. I have to admit, there *might* be something special about me, after all. (And I don't have to get my award sneaked to me from Roxie's winnings, either!)

Roxie is happy that I won, I can tell. She doesn't have the competitive edge like some of the dogs we watched on television at the New York dog competition. Those dogs spend their whole lives making sure every hair is perfect and they could jump at the drop of a hat. They're all special breeds. But I bet they never traveled to Africa before or sang with an elephant.

Roxie says, "I think it's the humans who make the dogs feel snobby about their breeds. All breeds have something to offer. Some are beautiful, and some are good at doing different jobs. But just like with people, it's what's inside that counts. And it's who you love, who loves you, and how they treat you. Somehow, winning a silly award makes me feel like a sage!"

I love it here in Africa. I am learning to be who I am and finding out who that really is. Maybe one day I will be brave like a wild animal too. I think about our elephant friend. He gave us water and he sang with us with his huge trumpeting voice. I bet he helps lots of animals and even humans. And he does it all from his heart—not to be in a contest or circus or to get some humans to like him. Yes, I'll remember this day forever. I kiss Mom's hand. And I blow a little chirp in Roxie's ear. She turns and looks at me with that big smile of hers. All is right with the world!

Roxie says, "I am very proud of you today and every day. Lots of photographers were crowding around you. I wish we could see those pictures!"

After ten days in the city, Kate finishes her meetings and feels content that making a new school *could become a reality*. After that, we hear a lot about her plans for the Elephant Matriarch School for Mothers and Children. "It will create community leaders and nature protectors," she likes to say.

We head back to our beach home. First, we stop off at an immigration office and get some official travel papers—in case anyone stops us again in the car. Luckily, we don't see that fat policeman again. We're getting to "know the ropes." We're on the lookout but we don't spot any elephants on the way back, either. Albert's brother, Edwin, is our driver. He says he doesn't have time to stop at the wildlife lodge.

We're hoping it won't be as hot back at the beach. Well, it is.

We're glad to be back in our familiar air-conditioned room—and running on the beach, accompanying Kate and Horace to outdoor restaurants, and playing with Amigo.

Every day as before, right after Kate gets home from her classes and when it's shady on the beach, we stroll there. We enjoy the ocean and the sand and become beach dogs. Our friends Jackie or Renson come with us and bring Amigo. We love to watch him dunk himself in the ocean and then roll in the sand. Sometimes Roselyn comes, and sometimes Horace comes, too. We sit with Kate as she watches the tide come in. Roxie sniffs and digs in the sand. I love watching with Mommie as the water "ebbs and flows." I hear her say that I have a poetic soul. She does, too.

The rainy season comes, and the weather cools off.

Chapter 15

ROXIE – Crab Mania

We discover little crabs on the beach. Most of them are not much bigger than my paw and they have see-through bodies. They're really fast as they run sideways. The beach seems to have little holes everywhere where they can slip right down inside. We think they're hilarious!

It's a great new game to find them and chase them. Sometimes, we don't see any crabs at all. We discover there aren't many to see in the afternoon—that they usually come out in full force in the evening. Kate laughs as we madly scamper after crabs, even when we're on leash. She runs with us as we race after them. They try to fight back and put out their little pincers to scare us off. I don't mind getting a little pinch now and then. That makes it more fun. Romie gets spooked and barks at them. It makes Mom laugh some more.

Romeo says, "They may be small, but those pincers could hurt your nose!" But soon he can't resist joining in. He runs after one. But when it stops, he barks at it to warn it not to bite him. Here comes another one, "Bark! Bark!"

I don't like Romeo's barking at first because I am afraid it will scare the crab away—and I want to catch him. But with

118

Mom laughing and his barking and the crabs running, sometimes I just join in with the barking and it's like one big game. But I tell Romie, "Even though it's a hoot, it's not nearly as exciting as stabbing him with my teeth."

We go out looking for them in late afternoon. Usually we see some, and the chase is on. In a few days, I am starting to catch them. I stop one and tap it with my paw. I'm not afraid of getting bitten. I tap him again. I push the little crab over on his back.

Next day I knock a crab on his back again and I realize *he can't run anymore! Heh heh!* I discover his Achilles heel, as Mom would say—a weakness he cannot overcome. Once on his back, he can't turn over. Next time, when I have one helpless on his back, I bite him. Then, I bite him again. Doesn't taste too bad.

"You *killed* him!" says Romie.

"Yes, and it's so much fun!" In the beginning, when I learn how to do it, I kill a whole bunch of them. It's when we're off leash and Mommie doesn't see me do it.

Romie says, "You get a big grin on your face. Maybe I wouldn't realize I am such a cowardly dog if I didn't live with such a brave huntress. Roxie, you look sweet and demure, but inside you are a brave warrior."

In the coming days, when we go to the beach, Mom tries to avoid the crabs, but usually we spot a few that she hasn't noticed and get a few hunts in. It is fun. Romeo decides he will keep trying and maybe one day, he will bite one, too. Mom loves seeing us jovial and playful, but she says, "Come on guys, I don't want you to harass the crabs. Crabs are special creatures. They live in their own world and they are great to see. I really don't want you to kill them."

"But Mom," I think as I give her my disappointed look, "It's so much fun. And there are so many of them." After that, we don't get to chase as many but we still do quite a few when she isn't looking. She lets us chase *one* crab on leash, and we can usually each catch one, but then she pulls us away before we can do it in.

Romie adds, "I still think that one of these days I will bite one."

Chapter 16

ROMEO – Done in by a Crab

One night, we return to Nomads. It's already getting dark. We're sitting under the table. Kate and Horace are getting a drink and we are eager to go down to the sand. We hadn't hunted for crabs down here before at the south part of the beach yet.

Finally, Mom takes us down to the beach while Horace waits for the food. We dash down to the sand, pulling her with us on our leashes. There are spotlights shining out toward the ocean, illuminating sections of the sand, and the sky is black. We dart like maniacs, looking for crabs.

Finally, we spot things moving in the shaded area. At first, we only see shadows. The critters who are running in the sand are so much *bigger* than the little crabs we were chasing up the beach. These critters are huge, round creatures, pink and orange, with long legs and big pincers!

"Oh, these are a different kind of crab! Look how big they are!" Kate says. Before I have a chance to think about it, Roxie takes off, pulling her leash as hard as she can, single-handedly hauling me and Mom with her whole fourteen pounds of determination. I join in the fun. The pink crabs are afraid of us. *Haha!* They all take off together in a big herd down towards the ocean. We all chase them and even Mom is laughing and whooping.

But Kate looks over at the patio and Horace is signaling to her to come back. Their dinner has been served. She says, "Uh oh. We have to go to the patio. We'll come back and see the crabs again after we eat our dinner. Don't worry. I'll bring you back." We are disappointed, but we go and patiently wait by her feet while she eats her tofu dish with vegetables and rice. I know that's what she's eating because she gives us a taste. After eating, she tells Horace, "I promised I'd take them back again to see the big crabs."

Horace says, "Okay, I'll have my coffee." He enjoys sitting by the shore and talking to the waiter, Gibson.

Roxie and I tear back to the sand. At first we can't see any crabs, but we search and search. Suddenly, we see a big group of them. Kate says a big group of crabs is called a *consortium.* Whatever they're called, the chase is on. They all take off and we're right on their tails! I'm having so much fun, I barely realize we've run right up to the water's edge. The crabs go into the surf, and Roxie follows without hesitation. The water is splashing at my legs, but my mind is on that crab. He won't escape this time! I'm barking loudly and feeling at the top of my game.

At that moment, the crab decides to stand up to me. Literally. He actually stands up tall on his hind legs! He's taller than me! His huge pincer is coming right for my nose! *Yeow!* I balk and back up on my hind legs. At that very moment, a wave comes in and pushes against us. I trip and I feel something *snap* in my leg. Instantaneously, I feel pain radiating from my leg. It feels like my surroundings go dark.

Kate can see there is a problem. She says, "Come on guys, let's go back." Problem is, I can't walk too good. Every step on my back leg is excruciating. I feel like such a baby. Mom says,

"It's okay. Let's take a little rest here on the sand." I lie on the sand with my two concerned ladies hovering over me. "Did you hurt your leg? Poor baby." She rubs it for me and it feels a little bit better. She carries me back to the dog bed under the restaurant table. It still hurts. But whenever I try to get up to walk, I get a shooting pain in my leg that travels up through my whole body. All I can remember is when I had this excruciating pain in my legs when I was a young puppy. I could barely walk at all. Managing that pain and finding something to eat were what my whole life was about on the streets. Dark memories. I really don't want to go back there.

Mom asks Horace to find a taxi. Usually, some are waiting at the front of the restaurant. She says we will walk very slowly and meet him there. She comforts me and whispers not to worry. She kisses me and says soon it will be better. And of course it is, I coach myself. I didn't have anybody to kiss me and reassure me when I was a broken puppy.

We get back to the apartment and she gives me a baby aspirin and some *arnica montana*. She rubs my leg and puts me up on the big bed. She puts Roxie up, too. We all cuddle around and *will* the throbbing to go away. Soon we all fall asleep. The next day, I don't feel too bad when I wake up. Mom tells me not to jump off the bed. She will lift me off. And she does ever so gently. As soon as I try to walk, I feel like I'm crumbling. Mom administers more aspirin and arnica. We all stay in most of the day. She and Horace take turns carrying me down the steps so I can sniff around in the back yard. Roxie stays by my side.

I don't want to suffer through another long injury or have to hop around for the rest of my life. I must fulfill my destiny and become brave. Maybe being brave is learning how to overcome your weaknesses. But how do I overcome a physical weakness? I bet I'm the only dog who philosophizes about his health. I must be a weirdo. But then again, Roxie loves me.

That gives me so much joy. Kate and Horace love me, maybe even more because I am different. Oh, too much time to think while stuck in the house like this. No long walks for a week or two—and especially no crab hunts. The leg still hurts. We go to see Dr. Oscar, our main vet. He tells us he doesn't have an X-ray machine. He says none of the vets here at the beach have one. It's because most people don't bring their dogs in for this kind of care. He'll have to take me to the people hospital.

Some people don't like dogs being allowed in the human hospital. We have to sneak in the back way when no one is looking. The man who takes the X-rays at the hospital—the radiologist—is afraid of dogs. I will have to go in and—if he is afraid of me—I will have to get sedated. That doesn't sound like something I will like. I know I better not growl or anything. I have to act brave. Kate and I ride with Dr. Oscar in his friend's car to the hospital. Roxie has to stay home with Horace because the X-ray guy doesn't like dogs. *Grrr!*

When we get there, the doctor has to make sure there are no other patients waiting to get in, then we sneak through the back door. Kate carries me into a tiny room with a hard table and a big machine to take pictures. We all crowd in. I vaguely remember something like this from my last X-ray. That time, the doctor wanted to cut off my leg! *Yeow!* I'm shaking inside. I try not to show it.

Dr. Oscar tells Mom she has to wait outside. As soon as she leaves, I feel a cold chill and a fear come over me. I bite my tongue and try not to cry. Suppose I will be in pain for months like I was before? Suppose I can't go hiking with Mom and Roxie anymore? Will they still love me? Will I be able to run again? The doctors put me on my back and pull my leg. It's very uncomfortable. I hear a snapping sound. It's all I can bear. I start to whimper. I want my *mom!* Where is Mommie? During my first leg injury I didn't have a mom—but now I *cannot* do without her! *Mommie!* They turn on the lights and

124

open the door, and Kate rushes in.

"Is he okay? I heard him crying," she says, as she sweeps me up in her arms.

"Oh no, he was a good boy. The X-ray is finished. He was crying because you weren't there."

We all look at a picture on the wall that looks like white lines on a black background. Dr. Oscar says it's a picture of me—my bones. He says it shows that my leg has a fracture in it, but that it has already begun to heal. I need to be careful, and it should completely heal. Oh, what a relief. I can't wait to get home and see Roxie's pretty face again.

Kate is relieved, too. It hurts, though. She says we'll be very careful and that my leg will get better and better. We're not allowed to run freely for a while, I have to take vitamins to help it heal.

***

Kate and Horace decide to take us for a long weekend up the coast where we won't have to walk around too much. A taxi van drives us and we stay in a different beach town called Watamu. We go to some outdoor restaurants and lull around the beach. We visit an old Arabic village that is hundreds of years old. We go to a turtle museum. It's all interesting and I don't have to walk very far. We celebrate Kate's birthday. She jumps and swims in the ocean and the rest of us wait on the shore.

Driving back down the coast, Mom says "Let's stop for lunch at one of those cute motels near Shimba Hills. I hear you can sit outside and it's very pretty." Before long, we're at a restaurant patio on top of a hill and we can see far away down in the valley.

Kate orders us some rice pilaf. I am gazing down into the meadows and forests. I have pretty good eyes. I see movement.

I keep staring. I see what looks like a group of elephants coming closer to us. I bark a happy alarm. Kate says we need to not make too much noise because there are other people having their lunch there, too. Horace stares into the valley.

"I think he sees something down there. Look!" Horace says as he points towards the elephants. We all stare.

"Oh, I think you're right. Look. It's a small herd of elephants! They're far away but they are getting closer," says Mom excitedly.

Roxie and I strain our eyes. As they get closer, we see what looks like two adult elephants, a medium-sized one, and two smaller ones all meandering slowly and browsing on trees. I feel goosebumps. The elephants look just like the ones we recently saw on video—and not that long ago, the ones we saw at the wildlife lodge. So peaceful and beautiful. They all seem so in sync with each other. Roxie and I especially like gazing at the little one on the side. He looks so tiny, but we know from up close he would be ten times bigger than we are!

The manager of the hotel comes over. He says there used to be lots more elephants that lived here, but conditions had become so dry that they had to migrate to other places. We were lucky to be able to spot this herd. I feel so connected to the elephants somehow, just like Kate does. I wish they all lived right next door. After lunch, we drive back home to Diani Beach, feeling wiser and more content for having seen more of Kenya and the incredible animals here.

The weeks go by and my leg is getting better and stronger. After a while, I almost forget all about the fracture.

Chapter 17

ROXIE – Wayward Adventure

It's getting near the time for Kate's big trip with her students. She raised some money from a charity club for the group excursion. She plans to rent a spacious, air-conditioned van for the girls and accompany them north towards the Tsavo National Park—where they could see elephants for the first time! That was near where we saw the elephants, too!

Most of the girls grew up in tiny towns and country areas, and these areas are where the farmers have clashes with elephants who are eating their crops. Many people who live in this area don't understand how important elephants are. In order to shoo the elephants away from their farms, they do dangerous things to them that may hurt or even kill them, like entrapping them in snares or shooting them with poison arrows. Kate wants her students to see the wild animals in their natural habitat so they will understand and appreciate them better, and she hopes then they would never consider doing such destructive things to them.

The young moms don't understand that elephants existed before dogs and humans. They used to live all over the earth. Only a few lucky people can see elephants today, and they must understand that elephants need help. Humans need to respect them and give them space. That's what Mom has been teaching the girls and us. Most of the students have never met an elephant, even though they live in the same country. It would be like living near the ocean and never seeing the water. We were able to come halfway around the world to see them and help them. I feel lucky that even though the girls never saw an elephant, Romie and I did. Not only that, but the bull elephant gave us a shower and he sang with us, like he wanted to be our friend. And we've also been able to see them in their peaceful communities.

Then there was that time we heard Kate say that she may have been *an elephant in another lifetime*. She saw herself as an African child whose mother was killed. She was rescued by a herd of elephants who became her family.

Romeo chimes in, "I think that would be so cool. But Mom can't remember it very well. Wouldn't it be great if you could remember all the things you learned in your previous lifetime? Maybe we have so many lifetimes that we just can't remember everything. I still love that story, though—the possibility of having another life—and even as a different animal. I wonder if it has to do with how well you live your present life?"

Romie rubs against me for some snuggle time. He says, "'Cause I think Roxie would become a queen!" He makes me smile.

***

Back at our apartment, we are once again surrounded by the vervets, Sykes, and colobus monkeys all swinging through the trees near our apartment. Kate says colobus are the only primate with no thumbs. So when the colobus monkeys jump and climb from tree to tree, you can see the branches shake. They can't get a good grip on the branches like the other monkeys.

I think about how I couldn't get a grip on that tree, either, when I was a puppy and I fell down right on that guy's beard! I wouldn't want to do that again. So I'd say, for having *no thumbs*, those colobus monkeys do alright for themselves. When the flowers are blooming, all the monkeys jump in the trees in front of our apartment and eat the flowers. Sometimes, they stay for a long while. So does their poo, which falls on the ground around the trees.

Kate and Horace are always telling us not to eat monkey poo, but there are *so many* monkeys, and they poop everywhere. I know it sounds gross, but for some reason their poo has a sweet taste—maybe something like the dark chocolate Kate likes. I don't know for sure, because she never lets me taste it. It's not healthy for dogs. When Mom isn't watching, Romie and I taste some monkey poo. When she catches us, she scolds us and pulls the poo from our mouths. Dr. Oscar says the monkey poo might be the cause of bad infections—just from picking it up or licking the stuff off the ground.

In California, I didn't notice much poo on the ground. Most dog moms and dads pick up their dog's poo with little plastic bags. There aren't any wild monkeys or their poo in California. But here in Kenya, people are not permitted to use plastic bags. Mom says that's a *good* thing because it helps save the turtles and fish in the ocean who could end up getting stuck in plastic.

One night, we get robbed. Mommie bought two pretty handwoven rugs for Romeo and me. When she and Horace take us to a restaurant, instead of bringing our dog beds, they bring the rugs so we can sit comfortably under the table. One night, the electricity is out and there's no light on the streets. As we're walking on the dirt road near our apartment, a guy on a motor scooter, which they call a *boda boda,* drives by too close to us. Romeo barks at him to go away. He circles around

130

and comes back again.

This time, the driver snatches the bag with the rugs in it right out of Horace's hand—and so fast, before we even know what happened. We're all shocked. I hear Kate and Horace say that it isn't the tourist season anymore, so many people around us are short on money to buy food. That's why there is more stealing. I know Mom and Grandpa are unhappy about being robbed. Horace says it can happen anywhere. But as far as we know, it hasn't happened to us or our friends in California. What if one day, the thieves snatch Romie or me? Then what?

I don't like living with that danger looming over us. Romie and I are getting a little homesick and we think that Kate and Horace must be, too. We know Kate is teaching young moms about elephants. But she doesn't get to see elephants that much. She's nervous about taking us places because we might run into crooked police and dog snatchers. She doesn't have many friends here, either, like she does at home. I think maybe she and Horace want to go home, but they need a little push. I wonder, what would she do if *I got sick*? It's just a thought.

The day comes when Kate takes her students on their wildlife expedition. She put together a weekend plan, and the girls will finally meet elephants. She talks about it all the time. While they're gone, she plans to take them to a lodge for a fancy lunch. Many of them have never eaten in a restaurant before.

***

Horace has full responsibility for us. He feeds us and takes us on walks. We have to stay on leash on our walks with him, except sometimes, we get to roam on the beach for a little bit. The only other time we are off leash is late at night, if one of us has to pee. We are allowed to run outside on our apartment grounds. Romeo prefers to hold it in, but I am curious and brave enough to run outside in the dark by myself.

The first night she's gone, I run down the steps and onto our back-yard lawn, and I find a little round porcupine poking along in the grass. He's only about half my size. I bark at him. Ami-go comes to see what's going on. Soon, Horace and Romeo follow. For some reason, Amigo and Romeo don't find him as fascinating as I do. I've never seen anything like him. One of the truly amazing animals of Africa.

Horace spots the little fellow. He tells me to leave him alone, but I just can't. Animal instinct is strong, even in us intellectual dogs. That's when Horace picks me up, and he carries me back up the steps. I'm disappointed I don't get to feel the little animal or bite him. Horace warns he could hurt me, but I don't think so. He's much smaller than me and moves really slowly. Horace tells me he has sharp quills, but I don't understand what that is. Maybe another night, I plot, I will run outside and find the little guy and try not to bark so loud. Then no one will be there to stop me from exploring him up close. Who knows what would happen from there?

The second day Kate's gone, in the late afternoon when we're going out for our walk, we hear Renson and Jackie talking about a sick monkey they had found in our yard. They think he's been poisoned. I don't see him anywhere.

That night, I stand by the front door and make some noise like I have to pee. Horace, half asleep, opens the front door and frees me to race down the steps to the backyard, where I search for the little porcupine critter.

I sniff all around in the grass near the place I last saw him, but I don't smell him at all. The grass is still wet from rain, and I stumble on a rock. I look back, and there, partially hidden under the big stone, I see a pile of monkey poo. *Tempting*. One smell and I learn it has lots of flavors. It's fresh and has a sweet-and-sour tang when I taste it. *Mmmm*. If Kate were there, by this time she'd be pulling me away. On my own, I'm free to investigate. I take another lick, then another. *Hmm*. I am a little hungry, so I let myself go and eat the whole pile. I look around. It's very dark out. No one sees me. *Heh heh!*

I take myself back up the steps and go lie down in my dog bed. Kate is supposed to come home the next morning. I fall deep asleep. The next thing I know, it's light outside and I hear footsteps coming up the stairs. *That must be Mommie!*

I jump up. My stomach feels achy. I make it almost to the door. It opens. In walks Kate, smiling and glowing. *She must have seen elephants*, I think. Suddenly—I don't know what's happening. I have the worst pain in my tummy ever.

When Romie gets sick, he becomes very still. I can't be still. I whimper and run around. I feel like I have to poop and throw up at the same time. I'm beside myself. What is happening to me? I'm making ugly noises. I want to die. I hear Romie whimper in concern. All my energy drains out of my body. Mommie picks me up. She takes me outside. I vomit and poop again and again. My tummy is raw. I feel dizzy and weak. This keeps up to the point of exhaustion.

I sense a blackness coming over me, like I'm falling asleep. As I am starting to pass out, I think, maybe when I wake up, we'll all be in California. Or maybe I'll see Mommie in her dreams like Marcello did. Romeo knows I love him. My thoughts are dazed and confused. Dr. Oscar comes to see me,

I think. It's all such a blur. They're giving me oils to make me poop even more, to get it all out of my system. It feels like I am on the verge. Everyone is panicky.

Chapter 18

ROMEO – Lost Without Roxie

I am helpless with Roxie so sick. I never leave her side.

Roxie, my sweetheart
My partner
My light
I need you now as on the first day
Your cleverness has always
been there
Your love of me has always
been clear
Roxie, I love you
Pull yourself out
Stop being sick
Come back!
Come back!
Come back!

Chapter 19

ROXIE – Petrified

I will recover. I am strong. I am female. Not to mention, a *warrior princess!* My dear Romeo keeps me company and lucky for me—he is always nearby. But he can't stop whimpering. I hear faded bits of conversation. Kate says she finally got her students to meet the elephants and that they all fell in love with them. They visited the Voi Reintegration Unit of the Sheldrick Wildlife Trust and saw the baby elephants drinking milk from bottles. The girls were overcome with joy, watching the babies drink milk, just like their own little ones do.

I want to know all about Kate's trip and hear about plans to go back to California. Kate promises to help Agnes and Mwaka, her oldest students who have been volunteering at Colobus Conservation. They are now about ready to leave the rescue center. She promises to sponsor them for college so they can follow their dreams.

Hari comes for a visit to discuss the Elephant Matriarch School. There is no school like it in all of Kenya, or maybe anywhere. Kate tries to gather support for it from the expats, but she says they are afraid to try something new. Hari promises to save money for the land for the school grounds so they can move forward. In order to accomplish their goals, Kate feels she needs to return to California to raise some money.

She tells Horace, "So maybe it's time to plan our departure—as soon as Roxie is feeling good enough to travel."

Horace agrees, "I will miss Kenya. For me, this is a once in a lifetime experience. I can see why people spend so much money to come here, even for a week or two. The local people are warm. And when you meet the wild animals, it is magical."

Romie says to me, "I finally understand the difference between wild animals and pets. The wild ones are their own personages, with their own kingdoms. They rely on each other and use their wits to find food and shelter and survive. I am proud to be in the animal kingdom. But I don't think I would like the wild life. After having a great human family, now I am so used to humans. I love their caring and comfort, the pampering and the feeling of being part of the same team.

"Although, elephants are something else. They have all the smarts and love and security they need. They make the earth beautiful. Elephants don't really need humans. But it's a good thing that humans can help elephants undo the harms they've been inflicted by other humans who have taken their land and stolen their babies for work and entertainment. It is only right that humans should come to their aid."

I also feel so proud of Kate and Horace for coming here to help them and bringing us on this adventure. I am overwhelmed with love for them. Roxie and I agree on that and give each other a kiss. We can feel that our exciting escapades here have only brought us closer together.

Kate and Horace make plans to buy plane tickets back to California. They say we can stop for two or three days in *Paris* on the way home! That's what Rick and Ilsa said they would always have in their hearts!

It sounds like fun. Every day, I'm better and better. Many things, for sure, I will miss about Kenya—Amigo, the monkeys, our apartment, Renson and Jackie, the ocean, the tuk-tuks, the crabs, the camels, the cows and goats, and, of course, the elephants. And we love all the African heroes we've met who are helping the wild animals. These two years have been the adventure of a lifetime.

But, still, it's different from home. Sometimes it's scary. The robbery, the rabies, the mean policemen, the heat—those things make us nervous.

It was a dumb thing for me to eat that monkey poo. I made myself sick. But I know I am a strong dog. I've been in tough spots before. Now we are talking about going to see dogs with fancy haircuts in Paris! We're making plans to go back home! *Any time now, the suitcases will be coming out! Heh heh!*

A week passes. The sun is shining brighter than usual. The air is pleasant and getting warmer again. It also feels like we may be headed toward another hot season. Kate is making phone arrangements for the long trip home. She and Horace are busy looking for tickets and checking the many requirements to be able to move around the country with us. We don't want to take any chances with policemen when we're traveling on the roads, or with airline people who we know can sometimes make our lives difficult.

***

Kate takes us for a slow walk into town so she can chat with a man who helps foreigners with their arrangements. There are a lot of people on the road today. As usual, we get many stares and people coming up to Kate, saying, "Give me one." Romie is making his low growl, and Kate is brushing it off, saying, "He's being protective."

From behind a lively gathering of shoppers, a man appears

and *swoops me up*. He entraps me with his muscular arm and takes off running really fast down the street with another guy who acts like his partner. I squirm and push and try to get away. His strong hands have a tight grip on my back. Romeo barks loudly. He pulls hard on his leash, running after us, hopping on three legs. Mom runs with him, screaming, "Stop them! Dog thief! Help!" Concerned strangers turn around. Some of them join the chase.

The thugs run toward a car parked near the gutter. They jump inside with me as their prisoner. The guy who isn't holding me starts up the car. It's all happening so fast. What's going to become of me?

Romeo is still barking and howling. In a flash, he pulls away from Mommie and he jumps higher than I have *ever* seen him do—through the open back window of the car! Kate shrieks.

Romeo is so worked up and angry, he's on fire. I don't think he even realizes or stops to think about what he's doing!

The car starts moving and nearly runs over a few local people who are trying to help us. It speeds down the road at a breakneck pace. We speed farther and farther away from our mother and protector, the only love and safety we've ever known. I've never felt so petrified in my life. I don't think any wild animal, big or small, could make me feel as fearful as a mean human.

Romeo growls loudly from the back seat, showing his teeth. He pushes his head between the front seats and tries to bite my captor. The guy hits Romie in the snout and he falls back. It must be painful because he whimpers loudly. Moments later, he somehow jumps up from where he is in the back seat, right onto the driver's head! The driver swerves the car. The guy who's holding me swings his left arm back and whacks Romie down. I gasp and squeak and hope he is okay. The guy looks at me and says, "Shut up!"

The car is speeding down the road, farther and farther away from Mommie. I am trembling in fear—and silenced by fear. I can't see how my Romeo is doing in the back seat. After a while, I stop panting. I gather my strength and start barking. Romie immediately joins in with the loudest wolf howls I've ever heard him make. He boosts himself right up to the driver's ears. He is so loud that the driver screams in distress. "Awwwwgh! Stop it! Shut up!" The guy holding me puts his hands over his ears. "Shut the hell up!" While he is screaming, he reaches back with one arm to whack Romeo. Poor baby! He whimpers and falls back down to the floor.

After catching his breath, he somehow manages to jump back up on the driver's head. The car veers to the right, makes a sharp turn, and the driver loses control. The car ends up in a ditch in the road. The man tries to grab me. I wiggle around him and squeeze back between the seats to join Romeo. That's when I see him sitting protectively on a pair of *elephant tusks* on the floor. *We've been captured by wildlife poachers.* We exchange knowing looks.

The man reaches back again, and Romie bites his hand. "Damn you!" The man whacks him across the face. Poor Romie! For once in my life, I'm so angry and upset, I can barely bark. *I've never in my life seen a more heroic dog.*

The driver manages to get the car started again and it lurches out of the ditch. We pick up speed. The car swerves sharply right, going momentarily out of control, and overshoots the road. The tires get stuck in some soft mud and the two guys jump out the door. While they try to pull the car out of the mud, we jump out the window and run as fast as we can in the opposite direction. I hear the faint sound of a police siren in the distance. The thieves drop what they're doing and run after us down the road.

At that moment, I think, we both get the same idea—to duck to the right on the side of the road and make a sharp turn into the forest. With the guys still on our tails, we dive in among the trees. We zigzag so many times, we lose our sense of direction. We're jumping over bramble and holes, which must be difficult on Romie's leg.

We head to the left and suddenly we realize we don't hear any footsteps. Maybe we've lost them. We're panting hard. We take a long look at each other. We hear the thieves yell something to each other. We take off again, running as fast as we can, noses to the ground. This is a matter of life and death. *Ours.*

Suddenly, there's a huge roadblock smack dab ahead of us in the middle of the forest. We look up to see what it is. At first we can't tell, but then we realize—it's the leg of a gigantic elephant! He is even larger than the one we made friends with at the waterhole who had those enormous tusks halfway to the ground. These tusks are actually *dragging* on the ground. We stop in our tracks, our hearts thumping out of our chests. I'm hoping and praying this elephant will be friendly. The whole world seems to stop. We stare up, open-mouthed.

Slowly, the elephant reaches down and fondles us with his long trunk. Our hearts skip a beat. Romeo makes a high-pitched sound of delight. The elephant responds in kind with a chirping sound. We pause and take it in. Our moment of reverie quickly ends when we hear the increasingly louder sounds of feet crackling on twigs and leaves.

Uh oh! Here come the crooks! They stop in their tracks. The elephant lets out a thunderous, trumpeting holler in their direction that practically blows them away. They take one look at him, turn, and dash, heading back out of the woods as fast as they can. The elephant goes charging after them, and we scamper behind. We all race back to the edge of the forest.

Another police siren is now coming in our direction and it's getting louder. A moment of relief. Sometimes you need the police! Most of them are not mean or crooked. When we get to the forest edge, we spot a motorcycle and a policeman on the side of the road examining the getaway car. As the thieves get back to the road, the cop pulls his gun and shoots in the air as a warning. Then he sees the elephant. He slowly backs up in fear. We come out of the woods and stand with the elephant. We feel his warm breath and then his soft trunk petting our backs. It feels like a little piece of heaven in the midst of the chaos. Lord of the jungle! Elephant! It's a moment I will never forget. As if time is standing still.

When Mommie tells us stories about elephants, she talks about how they sometimes help other animals. Who could imagine that an elephant would help Romeo and Roxie get out of such imminent danger? *The elephant is saving our very lives!*

Who would think Romeo could be such a courageous savior? As I look at him all bruised and sore next to me, it occurs to me—he came to Africa a skittish pup, and he's going to go home with the heart of an elephant. I feel my heart opening up and gushing out warm, loving feelings towards him. It feels romantic and exciting.

Surprisingly, the elephant makes a whining noise and backs up into the trees.

We see Kate jumping out of a tuk-tuk that was following the second police car. She runs towards us down the road, and we run towards her. Time seems to stop when we hear a huge *thud* in the forest.

The cops are running after the thieves. Kate is coming toward us.

Now, suddenly, Romeo is running *back into the forest. What the heck is he doing?*

The cops nab the two fugitives and tie their hands behind their backs. "This is what happens to elephant poachers!" Thank goodness—they must have found the tusks in the back of the car.

Mommie is wailing in happiness and relief. I stand frozen.

She suddenly shrieks, "Where's Romeo?"

We hear Romeo's voice moaning from inside the forest. His moaning turns into wailing and howling at the top of his lungs. Mommie grabs me and we cautiously proceed back towards the trees.

A policeman puts out his arms for us to halt. "It's dangerous to go in there—there's a big bull elephant."

Romie is still making loud moans. Kate says, "We *have* to go in—my baby Romeo is in there. My dogs are my children." She holds me tightly and we press onward past the cop. The policeman decides to escort us. Mom and I are both overcome with worry. I'm so terrified for Romie that my whole body wants to cry. We forge ahead with the policeman and try to tiptoe as we move towards Romeo's voice. We finally see him. He's pacing nervously next to the elephant, who is lying on the ground on his side.

The policeman says, "Call your dog. We need to get out as soon as possible."

Kate calls Romie sweetly. "Romie! Hi, Romie, look at you. You're so brave! Can you come for hugs and kisses? Come on, Romie! Come see Mommie!" He doesn't move. He stubbornly remains near the back leg of the elephant and continues to bark.

The policeman says, "Ma'am, this is a dangerous situation. We know about this elephant, 'Big Tusk.' He has killed a man—a poacher. I have to take you out of the forest now, before someone gets hurt."

Kate says, "Officer, believe me, there's a reason he's doing this."

"Romie!" she calls again.

Finally, Kate notices the reason why Romeo is refusing to leave his friend. There's a long arrow sticking out of the elephant's back leg, probably hurting him and causing him to fall down. "You are trying to get help for the elephant! Oh, my dog! You are the ultimate hero!" she cries.

"Officer, look! The elephant is wounded with an arrow in his thigh. It's probably a poison arrow. Call the rangers! Call the Sheldrick Trust mobile veterinary unit!"

The policeman seems dazed.

"This could be a lethal poison arrow! Please!" Kate urges.

The policeman nods and gets on his phone to call for help. Then, to Kate, "You know, I hear there was some recent crop raiding by elephants not far from here. The local farmers are trying to protect their crops."

"I understand. But did you get the rangers and a vet on the phone? Are they coming right away?"

"How do you know so much about it, ma'am?"

"I'm an elephant advocate and Environmental Director at AfricaGirls. This is exactly why we're here, to help rural people and protect elephants. We find ways to preserve their crops, too. We all need to work together to save this magnificent species."

The cop says, "Big Tusk is well known. One of the last big tuskers. He is in trouble and many will come running. The elephants are blessed with good luck to have you."

"And, also, good luck to have my *dogs*!" she smiles. Mommie reaches down and gives me a hug. She sits on a log, waiting. I wait near her. Romeo sniffs all around the injured Big Tusk. Romie is such a great friend to the elephants and it makes me love him all the more.

The policeman wants us to leave the forest. Romie will not budge, though, and Mom and I are determined to stay with him. The policeman tells us that if the elephant gets up, he could be a danger to all of us. Kate promises we'll leave if we see the slightest stir from the elephant. I feel nervous. He is, after all, the biggest animal on earth, and he has killed a person. But then again, we are his friends. He might not like the guy with the gun, though. While we are at a stalemate on what to do next, we hear the sound of an ambulance siren approaching. Thank goodness! Mommie sighs and gives me another hug.

We hear feet rustling through the leaves as two wildlife veterinarians and a ranger arrive in the forest. They find us pretty quickly. They examine the arrow. They tell us they must dart Big Tusk in order to fix his wound—and that we must all leave. Kate thanks them for coming so fast, and she grabs Romeo.

We all walk gingerly back to the road, where we wait. Everyone is pretty tense. While we're waiting, Kate thanks the police officers for being such great rescuers, too. "You helped save my darlings and I will be forever grateful to you. It's good to know there are some great police officers here." They shake hands.

In about half an hour, the doctors come out of the woods. They tell us they've removed the poison arrow from the elephant's thigh and his wound has been treated. They have put antibiotics and healing clay in the wound. They expect a full recovery. Big Tusk will be waking up from the anesthesia any minute. We must all get in our cars quickly before he does.

We do as we are told, and we walk swiftly back to the road and wait in the tuk-tuk.

We hear a great, howling trumpet sound from the forest. He's getting up. Everyone's on pins and needles. Big Tusk comes to the edge of the road where we all are waiting, and he stands still for a moment.

As soon as he sees him, Romeo jumps out of the tuk-tuk and he barks sharply toward the elephant. Big Tusk looks directly toward him and lets out one more thunderous, trumpeting sound that fills the air. It's like he's saying an elephant-sized thank you. Romie and I bark back at him enthusiastically. Then he turns around and quickly disappears back into the forest.

I remember that moment so well. Romeo no longer feels like my halting companion. I tell him, "Romeo, you are my superhero!"

We hear a car coming down the road. It's Horace arriving in a taxi. A neighbor alerted him about the kidnapping. Kate fills him in on the details. We all hug together and cry in relief and celebrate our wonderful Romeo. We need to get him home and dress his wounds.

Kate is right about elephants. They *are* worth traveling around the world to meet. Although they are the biggest, sweetest animals on earth, they need our help. Romie and I feel very proud that we have made friends with elephants, and we have helped them. If Big Tusk hadn't scared away the dog thieves, we might have been trapped in a horrible, life-threatening situation with those two criminals. Who knows if we would ever have seen Mommie again? It's almost too frightening to think about.

The elephants are lucky to have *us*, too. Romeo and I have helped to capture two nasty elephant poachers. Who knows how many more elephants they may have killed if we hadn't been there to help get them arrested? And most of all, if Romeo hadn't bravely stayed with Big Tusk, he might have died a sad and painful death from the poison arrow, all alone in the forest. If Kate hadn't known all about these problems and brought us to Africa to help elephants, there might not have been anybody around to call for help.

Kate says an enormous bull elephant like Big Tusk will be the father to many more baby elephants. By saving him, we are saving not just one, but many future elephants, too. It's perfectly clear to me now: The elephants wanted *all of us* to come to Africa.

Romeo says, "All the time we've been in Africa, we'd been learning to be more elephant—more caring—braver—in tune with the earth. The animals here *have* to be brave just to survive. I think their valor is rubbing off on us."

The elephant is the *ultimate* earthling. He's here not only to enjoy the earth, but also to save it and all of us animals. The elephant helps forests to grow and helps animals in trouble. He even helped *us*! I feel so happy that we could help him, too.

I love my mommie so much. If she hadn't seen my picture on the computer so long ago and adopted me, who knows where I would have ended up?

And Romeo! He is the bravest of heroes. He jumped in that car window to save me and he will always be my warrior prince! (As well as my Prince Charming! *Heh heh!)* As we ride to our apartment in the back seat of the taxi, we lean against each other all the way home. Poor Romie is scratched up and bruised, but even so, that night we all go to sleep with contented hearts.

Chapter 20

ROMEO – Honors and Recognition

We had a date to depart, but now there is a delay in our plans. Kate and Horace are notified by the governor's office the next day that they want to give us a citation. I'm worried it's because we did something wrong. Maybe because we didn't listen to the policeman at the forest when we ran back to the elephant? Maybe now they won't allow us to leave and go back home? (I'm secretly hoping that maybe that would happen. Now that we've met another great elephant, I'm yearning to meet even more.)

Maybe they want me and Roxie to work with rangers, since we helped catch those poachers? I'm not sure what it could be, but I'm a little anxious. Kate and Horace don't seem worried. She gives us both a bath before our appointment. She and Horace dress up nicely. We call a taxi.

When we get near the governor's office, we notice some of our friends are there, and they're all dressed up. There's Roselyn and Hari, and there's our other friend, Maria Luisa, and Nancy from Colobus Conservation. Some of Mom's students are there, too—Agnes and Mwaka, both with big smiles on their faces. What could this be about? We also see police or military guys with hats and fancy uniforms. Maybe they are going to award Kate for her work with the girls?

We all go inside the stately building to a fairly large room. There is a big man sitting at a desk with lots of flags around him. He salutes us as we go in. All the people have followed us inside the room. After his salute, most people sit down. Kate walks us up to the front. "This is Romeo, sir."

"Romeo, you are a treasure to our county and our country. I salute you for coming here and for helping our country. You helped save one of our last big tuskers who was wounded, and you wouldn't leave him alone until help arrived."

I get excited and spin around.

The governor goes on, "I understand you have also rescued your companion dog, Roxie, from criminals. In doing so, you have helped us catch the two most notorious elephant and rhino poachers in Kenya. We have been on their tails for years.

"You are the bravest dog I have ever met. And is this your

girlfriend, Romeo?" he says, smiling at Roxie. Suddenly, there are chuckles and claps from the audience. "I wish to give you both medals." He puts one around each of our necks. Everyone claps.

Mom looks at us and says, "Do you want to sing a thank you for him?"

I look at Roxie and she smiles. She starts with little yaps, and I join in with my wolf howls. We escalate our sounds, and here we are, back to our song again! Someone takes our photo and says it will be in tomorrow's newspaper! I never thought that would happen! We do one more round of our famous duet. We look at each other and smile.

Chapter 21

ROXIE – Parisian Surprise

Since we have to change the day of our departure, we must wait yet another ten days for our plane ride. I guess we need the rest. Living through all the high energies and traumas of our dognapping, poacher-catching, and elephant-saving makes it feel like another whole year we've been in Kenya. Romeo says, "My wounds are healing quickly. I wouldn't change them for the world."

We both cry about leaving our African home. We could never meet so many animals at home in our whole lives as we can see here in one week. I know we'll miss them all for sure—even the monkeys. It's comforting to know that there are so many great animals in the world—animals that most dogs don't ever get to meet. Hopefully, we're taking a little bit of them home inside of us. And we adore Jackie and Renson and Amigo and the others who have given us so much love.

The days pass slowly. Packing up our belongings, giving away lots of things, selling other stuff, weighing suitcases. It's a long process. I nearly forgot how long it took us to get here when we started out. Back then, I wasn't aware of all the preparations Mom had to go through. Tomorrow, the neighbor who wants to buy our television will pick it up. Tonight, Kate and Horace are watching it one last time. It's one of their favorites again tonight—*Casablanca*. I perk up when they talk about Paris. That's where we're going in two days! "Here's lookin' at you, kid!"

We are finally ready to leave. It's been almost two years, I think—since we flew on a plane. Horace found a special deal for us to ride in business class, but we find out when we get on the plane that the seats are in the middle. One thing that helps my travel queasiness is putting my head out the window or at least looking out the window. Now I can do neither. We are off to a rough start. I felt like a brave warrior in Africa, but I'm no match for Air Europe.

The flight attendant insists that Romeo and I have to stay on the floor. Kate knows we are both nervous. They never made us do that before. As soon as she walks away, Mommie pulls us off the floor for hugs. The plane starts slowly, then comes to an abrupt stop, jerking us back and forth. My stomach is churning, and I am panting. I don't care about going to Paris anymore. I want to be in a comfortable, secure place and not on an airplane. Kate gives me a pill and I calm down.

Finally, we arrive in Paris. We make it through customs, and Romie and I are both eager to get outside and pee. It's cold and raining. In fact, it's *freezing*. I have chills up my spine. Most of the cabs at the airport *do not want to carry dogs* and leave us waiting on the curb! This is a far cry from our life in the tropics, where it's warm and *everyone wants us*. Our bodies are used to the African heat. Here, we are standing in the icy cold, shivering. Finally, a nice driver will accept canines, and he takes us to our Airbnb studio apartment. The minute we get out of the car, he gets a cloth and small vacuum to clean up after us. He must think we're dirty dogs!

Our lodging is very small, and we can barely crawl around

all our suitcases. At least we made it. I keep hoping it will warm up. Mommie did not pack our winter jackets when we left California, and, as much as we don't like wearing them, we could sure use them now. Kate and Horace had thought Paris was dog-friendly, and she says it has a reputation for being good for dogs. But the friendliness is sporadic. Some restaurants welcome dogs, but many do not. Some parks allow dogs, but they are few and far between. Dogs are not allowed in museums or on city buses. There are lots of places we can't go—and it's raining nonstop.

Mom tries to cheer us up. "We'll go shopping. We'll find you some cute Parisian jackets to warm you up!" The next day, we search for a store with dog clothes. Luckily, Horace speaks some French and we finally make our way to a store, soaking wet. We find some new sweaters and coats. Romie still does not like shopping, and he is impatient.

We go on a sightseeing bus. We get to sit on the top level in the front row. In front of us is an enormous glass window, and we can look down on all the streets and parks and people— and the unending rain. We get off at one of the tourist sights. We ride on the *bateaux* up the Seine River. Romeo enjoys it, but the motion distresses me, and I can't wait to get off.

That afternoon, Kate reads about a little church where they're conducting their annual "Blessing of the Animals" on the following day. She says people can bring their special animal friends to a church service, and it might be an interesting thing to do. We can receive a blessing and have a chance to meet some Parisian animals. At night, she gives us a warm bath, brushes our teeth, and brushes my long hair.

It sounds like the rain is stopping. I'm starting to feel hopeful and enthusiastic about the next day. Romeo and I are both getting excited.

We get up early and walk across town. We have far to go, and Mom knows Romie's leg is hurting. So we find a taxi for part of the way. The church is close to the Palais du Luxembourg. It is my favorite part of Paris, since it has that great garden we spotted from the tour bus. So many animals are here, lining up to get a blessing. Lots of dogs, some cats, and we see a calf and two goats! We rejoice. We didn't know if we would ever see these kinds of animals again once we left Africa.

There is a short, round-faced priest who speaks mostly in French but some words in English, too. He talks about how beautiful we all are and how *lucky* humans are *to have us* animals in their lives! I never thought about it that way. I always feel that I'm lucky because I have humans who love me and give me a great home.

We take our turn with the priest, who raises his arms as he prays and reaches down to pet us. He looks at me and Romie directly and says, "I can see that you two are very close, and you love each other very much. Is this true?" We look at each other. We stare into each other's eyes. We both feel so in love. The nice priest sees this, what we already know to be true. Kate nods *yes*! He says, "This is a special day, as we have permission to walk to the fountain in the Palais du Luxembourg next door. It will be a celebration to express Paris' love for her animals. I would like your permission for your two dear companions to be at the very front of the line."

I look back at Mommie. She has a wide smile on her face. "That sounds lovely!" Kate tells him, "Yes, Father, I think we would all like that very much."

"Okay. After this service, we will invite all the animals and their people to come with us as we walk next door to the *jardins*. We will have a lovely, short prayer by the fountain. I'm sure there will be some photojournalists there. Ça va? Sound good?" The priest blesses us for a healthy and happy life. We already have that. This seems like a good way to celebrate it.

As we're walking from the church back to the garden, Kate buys some flowers from a vendor, and she starts weaving them together. She is making flower collars for Romeo and me to wear! Kate tells us, "This is our special day in Paris! We will always remember it." Romie and I romp in the garden by some pretty flowers and shrubs for a few minutes, then we look up. We see groups of animals coming toward us from the church. Even the goats and the calf are coming!

Mommie says we can walk around a little, as the priest is not there yet. He must finish performing all the animal blessings in the church first. So we run around, saying hello to the dogs. Out of the corner of my eye, I see a tall Frenchman with a pipe and a beret. He's walking patiently in line with a little dog. They catch my eye because the little dog looks just like *me*!

Romeo sees them, too, and nudges me—and we go over to the dog. My heart skips a beat when I realize the dog is a dead ringer for *Rex*! My heart is thumping out of my chest. I go over to him. *Rex!* The Frenchman smiles and says, "Oh, hello. This is my dog companion, Jean-Pierre. You two look very much alike, *n'est-ce pas*, Jean-Pierre?" Jean-Pierre looks up at his dad.

I don't care what he says. I know it's Rex. *I should know my own brother!* I back up, feeling shy. Kate steps in. "*Bonjour, Monsieur*," she says, "*Oui*, they do look alike, *non*? You know Roxie here has a twin brother in California. They were both rescued by a shelter."

"*Vraiment*?" the Frenchman asks with interest. "Hello, I am Antoine. *Enchanté, madame*. Jean-Pierre is *also from California*," he says, pointing to Rex.

Mommie gasps with excitement. "*Really*? How very nice to meet you, Antoine. So Rex—I mean, Jean-Pierre—is originally from California?"

Antoine says, "Yes, five years ago, I was in Southern

156

California, and my associate took me to an adoption fair for dogs and cats. I wasn't looking for one, really. These were dogs and cats who had been adopted from a shelter and then returned for whatever reason. I went with her out of curiosity. That's where I saw Jean-Pierre, and I fell in love." By this time, Rex is wagging his tail. I am nudging and jumping on him.

Antoine looks down and sees the reunion going on between us. "*Mon Dieu!* I believe you may be right!"

Rex is jumping all over me at this point. The two of us start barking. We even have the same bark! We bark and bark! It's a hoot!

The priest is making his way to the front of the line. Kate calls him over and explains to him what's happening. The priest chuckles. "God works in mysterious ways with animals—and with good people." He winks.

Before I know it, Kate is putting flower garlands on me and Romie, and by now she has also made one for Rex. We walk up the two steps to the top of the fountain. Animals and their people have all gathered around. My heart is thumping.

"Today, we gather to celebrate many beautiful souls who have been chosen by their guardians for love and companionship," says the priest. "Let this be a beacon to people all over the world to love and care for our wonderful animals of every sort." Lots of people clap and shout, "*Oui!*" and "*Bien sur!*"

The sun is shining. A pretty butterfly flies right over our heads. The priest takes out his little ball and showers us with holy water. Romie looks at me. I know for sure he is thinking of the shower we got from the elephant. The priest swings his ball toward all the animals. I spontaneously bark with joy. Romeo accompanies me, and we create one of our best duets ever. His tenor voice is lilting and long-winded. I hear Rex join in from the crowd. Many animals join us in song. There are honks and yelps, meows and baas, and even chirps. *It is the most beautiful song in the world.* The people clap and shout "Bravo!"

Photographers take our pictures. Some people and their pets approach us and say hello, and they want to know more about us. It turns out a few of them have heard about us before—because we helped save the elephant! Kate says it must be in international newspapers.

I see Rex—I mean, Jean-Pierre—and Antoine inching closer to the fountain. Romeo greets Rex and puts his paw on him. Antoine giggles. Kate hugs the priest and thanks him for such a wonderful ceremony. We slowly walk away.

Antoine says he will be coming back to California on business soon, and perhaps he will bring Rex, who is now wagging his tail. Kate tells Antoine that he and Jean-Pierre are most welcome to visit us and that we would love to see them again. Rex and I take one long last look at each other and bark in unison.

***

Our plane leaves that evening for the United States. On the way to the airport, we pass the Eiffel Tower, all sparkly and full of lights. I wish we could stay longer, although it seems like *nothing* could beat this wonderful day. Getting on the plane is easy. This time, everyone expects and welcomes us. The attendants give us a big middle seat between Kate and Horace!

As Romie and I kiss on the plane, I look over at our film-buff family, who are contentedly looking for movies to watch on the tiny airplane televisions. I gaze at Romeo. This day has been the most stupendously superb way to end our journey—to celebrate being animals, and to be celebrated. To be honored by Paris! And to be recognized again for our bravery! Not to mention finding Rex! It could be our happiest day ever. I believe we are all thinking the same thing for sure—for the rest of our lives, "We'll always have Paris!" *Heh heh!*

Chapter 22

ROMEO – The Spiral

We're back home in Santa Monica. It's been a few weeks now, and it feels comforting to be home where we can chill out in our own familiar space. It feels so private here without Renson popping in to fix things and without hearing Jackie's voice from our patio. Yet those things had started to become so familiar, too. In a way, there is a touch of loneliness, and maybe isolation, even though we are all together. However, I enjoy the quietness, and it's great to have our own car, so no more calling cabs or hailing tuk-tuks to go places. Our government medals and our dog show ribbons are now proudly displayed in the living room.

But at this moment, we are all focused on the state of Roxie's health. She is coughing, shivering, and can barely eat or move. Dr. Baum diagnosed her condition as pneumonia and gave her some meds. But there's some mysterious, nasty-looking stuff clouding up her X-ray. The vet is puzzled about it and recommends further consultations with specialists. We've already visited two other vets, and they're also stumped.

Roxie's throat hurts her so much, she can't even swallow

food. We spend hours at dinnertime while Kate works to find something Roxie can ingest. I have never seen the likes of these new foods, including puddings, puppy mush, and even cat food! Kate is trying to get Roxie to eat this stuff so she'll gain back some weight. I'm not allowed to eat them. I'm not complaining. But you know how we canines can be—always curious about new tastes and smells.

My energy is sinking as well, though I do nothing but rest. It's probably just a meltdown from all the high emotions and situations and travel we've lived through for the past two years. Roxie's problems are much worse than mine. I concentrate on her.

**

I haven't minded getting toted around to all these veterinarian offices as much as I used to. They still give me the heebie-jeebies, I must admit. Even though my heart yearns to give moral support to my dear Roxie, another part of me pulls me into fight-or-flight mode. Since Roxie is almost like a part of my own body, I will tolerate new places, waiting rooms, and any other inconveniences necessary so we can get her back to health. Besides her attempting, mostly unsuccessfully, to get Roxie to eat, Kate spends all her waking hours talking on the phone to experts about Roxie's condition, including dog communicators, psychics, and homeopathic doctors. This devotion is one reason I'll never budge from my little family. It's a warm ocean around me. As a young puppy, I had already learned what it's like to be outside that ocean. This reflection makes me realize I must be getting to be mature compared to my early days. Wouldn't I be a grand old pup with stories to regale his young ones with—if I had any. I'm hoping that maybe these journals will travel to the right ears, ones that will garner a thing or two from our experiences.

We're back from an appointment with yet another specialist who acts concerned and does more tests but basically doesn't seem to have a clue what to do for Roxie. We're relaxing in our comfortable dog beds. Roxie moans. "I can hardly breathe. I can't control my mouth. It goes up and down by itself. My neck hurts. I have no energy. What is happening to me?" Roxie lets out a tiny gasp. This is especially sad, as I have never heard her whimper or complain before this, even when she got sick in Kenya. Roxie is my rock. Even though she, too, was a young pup on the streets, she has always had the valor of a warrior princess. I feel helpless. We both nod out.

It's dinnertime. We hang out in the kitchen. Roxie is wheezing and shaking again. Kate hugs her and pets her. Then come all the potential foods she pulls out for Roxie. Mom opens some new cans she picked up at the vet's office. "Let's see if these go down," Kate says and tries to act cheerful. I can tell the stress of watching Roxie wither away is piling up on her, too. I lie down in the corner and try to relax.

When I open my eyes again, Kate is telling Roxie, "You're my best girlfriend! My brave girl! You ate a few bites. That was very good!" She gives her a hug. "We'll go out to the front for a short walk, then we'll all cuddle together. Does that sound nice?"

She looks at me and remembers she forgot to feed me. "Hello, handsome," she coos to me. "I haven't forgotten you. You've got something special, too!" She pulls out some leftovers from last night's vegan lasagna. *Mmmm*. She knows she has my attention now. She warms it in the microwave. I lap it up greedily. One of my favorites!

Then she gets us primed for our short walk of the day. Poor Roxie looks like she will fall asleep standing up. It's good to get outside and we walk slowly around the block. Roxie looks slightly invigorated. She and I go up to our bedroom dog beds. Shortly, Kate comes into the room to check up on us. She curls up with us on the rug and we all snuggle together. Roxie and I always enjoy cuddling. Kate hugs us and sings to us. It's the most comfort two sick dogs could enjoy. We close our eyes. Back in dreamland.

The next day, I wake up next to Roxie. I start to wonder, is Roxie getting weaker? We've been to three doctors and a hospital, and she is still sick. No one knows what to do for her. I hang around while Mom again tries to feed her cat food and treats, eggs and just about anything a dog might like. Roxie is so hungry. She tries for a bite but can't make herself swallow. Her throat must be closed off somehow, Kate says.

What's wrong, my sweet Roxie?

Later, Mom and Grandpa prepare a sack of fluid. Kate holds Roxie on her lap and Horace hooks the bag onto a door so the fluids will drip down. He squeezes the needle tip into Roxie's upper back. Mom holds her snugly. Roxie is a good patient. We all hang in limbo, waiting for the fluids to go inside Roxie. There is some soft music playing and we each go inside to our own little private spaces while we wait.

When Roxie has taken in the fluids, her eyes do look brighter. She looks around the room like it was a new place. Her eyes alight on the statue of Marcello. She says, "Marcello— I wonder where he is now." I thought he had passed away.

"Yes, he passed but his memory is still here and the things he taught me I still remember." She suddenly feels like reminiscing.

"Even though Marcello's joints hurt him and he couldn't see like he used to, he always held his own. He was a fierce protector of Kate. I started to help him whenever I could. Marcello and I looked out for each other.

"He taught me a lot of things, including getting to know the nuances of different humans we meet. I used to ignore most humans, unless they were my *important people*—like my family. In my old life with Rex, we didn't have much to do with humans at all. But Marcello showed me that every person is unique. He could understand and react differently with each one. Some new people he automatically would tease, knowing they were playful. Others he disliked right away, and he might even try to *bite* them.

"He would stop to smell the flowers. By observing him, I saw that he was *right*. I *was* missing a lot by seeing humanity as 'not important.' I also realized how pretty the flowers are. And Marcello did lots of tricks, too. He could do them all—no problem—as long as you had treats to offer. *Up, down, sit, roll over, bow, stay, hold food on your nose, find the ball*—those are a few of his tricks. But if there were no treats, he would do no tricks.

"At first, I didn't even know what a treat was. Soon, they became an indispensable part of my life, as well. Before I met Marcello, I was shy around humans and uncomfortable. After I watched him in action, I also became friendlier to nice humans."

"Wow," I tell her, "I thought you had *always* been friendly and charming. I'm learning more about you all the time. I've learned so much of *my* friendliness from *you*, from what you learned from Marcello. So, in a way, Marcello has been *my* teacher, too."

Roxie says, "Marcello and I became very close after he lost his eye. I stayed near him and looked after him all the time. When he died, there was a hole in my heart for my special dog friend. I doubted if I'd ever have one again. I felt more and more sorry for myself—and lonelier than ever. Kate mourned and was gloomy for a few weeks and cried a lot. Marcello meant so much to her. She said he 'opened her heart' to all animals. She felt bad that he suffered at the end of his life.

"But one morning, Kate woke up, and she said, 'Marcello came to see me last night in a dream. I saw him standing on our street corner and he was all dressed in golden robes. He was glowing. He looked serene and regal. I think he wanted me to know that he is in a happy place. He wanted us to move on with life.'

"After that, Mom didn't cry every day as before. She smiled again. Her dream of Marcello helped us all to be able to move ahead with life."

I say, "Wow, that's really incredible."

Roxie looks at his statue. "All hail Marcello! Maybe we'll all meet again in some other time and place."

I tell her, "I sure hope so. And I hope Kate is there, too. But *you're not dying.* No one is dying. We'll just have to find a smart doctor to show us how to get you better."

Roxie smiles. "Of course, the 'moving ahead' meant finding *you*!"

Chapter 23

ROXIE – New Hope

Kate calls us to come downstairs. We have an appointment with a new vet specialist. Maybe he'll figure out what's wrong with me. We slowly walk around the block first, then all get into Horace's car.

When we get to Dr. Feldman's office, he reviews all the charts. He suspects that I have picked up a serious parasite in Africa, and he gives me an X-ray and a poo test. Kate tells him that if I have caught a bug, it was likely that Romie might have it, too. So, he gives Romeo a poo test, too. He will have to send it to a special lab that can test for this parasite. Dr. Feldman seems intelligent and caring. Meanwhile, I still haven't eaten much and have gotten so skinny. He gives us some special nutrients to take home.

The next day, the phone rings. After a short conversation, Mom blurts out, "Dr. Feldman got results from the tests. Nothing showed up in Roxie's poo—but they found *dung beetle parasite* in *Romeo's* poo." That was a big surprise, since, compared to me, Romeo was feeling okay. It was the parasite that the doctor had suspected.

Dung beetle parasite is one of the most lethal parasites in

all of Africa and parts of Asia, he told her. Since Romeo tested positive and I have symptoms, he feels it's a good bet to move forward with the parasite medicine cure for both of us. It consists of taking heavy-duty pesticide medicine every week for six weeks.

Kate and Horace talk about pesticides in food. Horace says, "They're very dangerous and could even cause cancer—but since Dr. Feldman says it's the *only* thing anyone has found that would kill the dung beetle parasite, I think we should try it."

Kate says, "We don't really have any other good options. As a kind of bonus, Dr. Feldman says the dogs would go down in veterinary history as the first two American dogs recorded to ever have this parasite." Of all the awards we have or could achieve, *this is definitely my least favorite*. But it's a glimmer of hope, to say the least.

We have to send for the medicine, and meanwhile, we are to keep up with the present protocol of supplements and fluids for me. I am still suffering with symptoms and Romie is bored of being always in the house. But he tries his best to cater to me and keep my mind off things. He feels it is his job. "So, Roxie," he asks, "what happened after Marcello passed away?"

I will tell you—soon after seeing Marcello in her dream, Mommie started talking about getting another dog. She wanted to make sure it would be *someone I would like*. She told me, "I know you like to flirt with the short-haired terriers and smallish dogs. You don't seem to like dogs with long hair. And you definitely like boy dogs better than girl dogs." *She knows me better than I know myself*. Mommie and I have a special connection—a heart-to-heart energy. I feel hers and she feels mine. She understands me so well. But I didn't think we could find anyone to replace Marcello.

Next thing, she started looking on her computer at pictures of dogs. She said she wanted to find another Jack

Russell or Jack Russell mix who was younger than me. She was viewing pictures of dogs who needed homes, just like she did when she found me. I had never thought about it before: *How come* she wandered into *that* shelter, which was not very close to her home, and she knew *right away* she wanted to meet *me* and not any of the other dogs? My ears perked up.

She told me a story about my big eyes—looking right at her through the camera. And how she couldn't resist me. She said, smiling at me, "I was looking at so many dog pictures, and even though there were lots of cute dogs, I was looking for a very special one. It took many days of looking before I finally saw *Roxie's* picture. One day I looked, and there were these big, curious eyes looking right back at me. They were so adorable and intelligent. I felt right away I just had to meet this wonderful dog." She petted my head and looked directly into those eyes of mine with a wide smile on her face.

That was a shock! I didn't know I had beautiful eyes. I definitely didn't see *her* when I looked at the camera. I loved that story and hoped she'd tell it again and again. She knew I was enthralled, so she went on, "It's funny how you can look at hundreds of pictures, but then somehow the *right* one pops out at you." I cooed and swooned like an ingenue. I kissed her hand. She leaned down to kiss my face, and I kissed hers again and again. "I love you, too, Mommie." I sent her my message through our strong heart connection. My body quivered like melting butter. And so did hers. *Our hearts were one.*

We continued our search for a boy dog that we would all love. Mom says she was *sure* we would soon find the *right* dog to be a new member of our family. She searched for days. She even went out to homeless dog shelters and animal rescues to meet dogs. She still didn't find the *right* one. One day, Kate saw a picture on the computer of a dog she really liked. "Isn't he adorable!" She held me up to the computer screen to show him to me. But it was kind of like the camera. I didn't see clearly what was in front of me. All I could see were tiny boxes with pictures of hundreds of dogs—so really, I couldn't see much at all.

"He's with a rescue group. I'll contact them," she told me. She had to fill out some forms, which she did and sent in right away. Days went by, and we didn't hear back. Kate tried to call the rescue group a few times. No one answered. As long as she was looking, her spirits were high, and she was more fun to be with. Since no one ever got back to us from the rescue group, she searched on the computer again and found another possible candidate. "Aw, look at this other one. He's kind of sweet-looking." She called the people who had him, and they said, yes, he was available. They were far away, but Kate thought it'd be worth the trip.

So, we planned to drive up to this faraway place on Saturday and meet the second one. Thursday rolled around. Kate still had a strong feeling about the first dog. "I wish we could find out about the other one. Let's try again." This time when she called, I heard her say, "I have called you so many times and sent in an application for Skippy. We had a Jack Russell for sixteen years, but he recently died, and we have another little terrier who's lonesome. We really like your Skippy. But since I haven't heard back from you, we're going to meet another dog on Saturday, and we'll probably end up taking him instead."

A half hour later, she got a call. They wanted to bring us Skippy.

"Oh! Oh! Yes! Yes!" Mommie chirped. "Please come over! We'll be here this evening."

I ask Romie, "Did you know we were talking about you, Romeo?"

Romie smiles, "I was hoping you meant me! *Haha!* I remember that day very well! The foster lady who took me on walks got a phone call. 'Yes, I'll get him ready. We'll be all set

by six o'clock.' She came to my cage and took me for a quick walk.

"There was a knock on her door, and it was Ricarda! She was the one who believed in me, who saved me. Oh, I *loved* Ricarda! Maybe she'd take me home with her this time. I *knew* she liked me! I started to imagine all kinds of wonderful things. We went for a ride in Ricarda's car. My toes and paws were crossed. My heart was thumping. I tried to relax in the carrier.

"Finally, we got out, and Ricarda walked me on a leash. I was wondering if she realized how well I'd finally learned to walk on one of those things. I wasn't limping much anymore, either. We went up to a door, and she knocked. A dog was barking on the other side. The door opened. I saw an adorable little white dog with long hair and big eyes. (Guess who that was? *Yes, you, Roxie!*) You looked so delighted to see me! We stared at each other for a minute, and both of our tails were wagging back and forth.

"I looked up, and there was Kate! I knew she was my Mom from the very first minute. She welcomed me with a huge smile and her arms outstretched. (I remember every minute so well!) 'Look at you!' She told me. 'Aren't you adorable! You're so handsome!' She picked me up and gave me a full-body hug. She smelled like strawberries. I felt like I was in heaven.

"'He's beautiful!' I heard her tell Ricarda. 'I love him

already!' She patted and stroked me and couldn't stop smiling.

"Kate and Ricarda talked, and Mom showed us around. No cages anywhere! Did I die and go to heaven? Meanwhile, my new friend, Roxie, and I flirted and smiled. Kate said, 'Why don't we take them to the schoolyard down the street? They can run around a little. We'll see how they do.' Soon, we were all walking together down the street, each of us dogs on a leash. For the first time in my life, I had a posse, a family! *I hoped.*

"We got to a large yard with grass and went inside the gate. You and I were allowed to run off leash! I ran and I ran as fast as I could. Finally, I thought, 'My legs are working great! Wow, can I run!' I chased you and you chased me. I was so fast! I was so happy! I was in love!"

I pick up the story...

Yes, Romie, I remember every little detail, too, my sweet! We all walked up the street together, after you and I were running and running out in the children's baseball field while Mom and Ricarda were talking. We all came back to the house. Then the very best thing happened. The lady said goodbye, and she left you with us!

I looked up at Mommie, and she was smiling, too. We know a sweetheart when we see one! We were both falling in love with our young prince. My sadness was fading away. I felt her inner happiness and she felt mine. Both of our hearts were singing.

At this point, Romie and I snuggle up and breathe together, lost in the reverie of our first meeting.

Chapter 24

ROMEO – Emotional
Roller Coaster

Several days pass and our medicine finally comes in the mail. We swallow our pills as instructed.

The most wonderful thing happens! Roxie starts to feel a lot better after just a few days! She stops having spasms around her mouth, and her appetite comes back! The pesticides don't bother or upset her stomach at all. I, however, am a different case altogether. While I hadn't noticed any symptoms before, taking the pesticide medicine makes me feel nauseous. I don't feel like myself. My good mood is shaken by the negative feelings in my body. I sulk.

Every day, Roxie feels better and I feel worse. Kate calls Dr. Feldman about it and he says some dogs experience different reactions to medicines. He suggests she give me some *nux vomica* homeopathic doses, and she does. They do help a little. I can't believe I will have to go through this for six long weeks. *Ehhhhh!*

As Roxie feels cheerier and more energized, she notices that I am feeling low. In the second week, she is eating almost full-sized meals. I am picking at my food. She comforts me sweetly like I comforted her. We end up doing a kind of reversal of our previous weeks. She stays nearby and frequently lies close beside me.

For fun, Mom turns on the television and we watch reruns of the Westminster Dog Show. We like to make fun of the fancy dogs and laugh at them. For the first time, we also feel a little sorry for those dogs. To them, winning the contest is their whole life. When they don't win, some of them get so disappointed. We know how they feel. In our limited experience as show dogs, we experienced a bit of the highs. But we both are reminded of how, when we didn't win, it was not a big deal. We still felt like winners who had a great family and felt cherished. We had experienced many adventures that most dogs wouldn't even dream about.

We see an ad on TV for the ASPCA. What a contrast from the shiny manicured dogs in the dog show to the bedraggled ones in the shelter. Roxie and I look at each other knowingly— we realize we have become very knowing dogs. We've experienced the worst and the best. We've come out on the other side. We know love, and we also share a love for all animals, thanks to our wonderful mom and all she has taught us. Our hearts have gotten bigger and bigger.

We remember Big Tusk. I picture him foraging in the jungle and being a father to lots more baby elephants. There will always be a special place inside of me for the elephants. The elephants are independent and know how to take care of their babies. Just knowing they exist makes me feel good.

Days go by and I'm feeling more like my old self. Dr. Feldman wants us to come back to the office to get X-rays of our throats and chests. Roxie's previous X-ray showed she had had parasites nesting in her throat. He wants to check me as well. Kate takes us for the checkup. It turns out, Roxie is doing incredibly well. No more parasites in sight. As for me, there are no visible parasites, but there is a little mark on my X-ray which the doctor needs to examine with the radiologist. We must wait around.

When the doctor comes out, he speaks seriously to Kate and Horace. "Both the dogs are doing very well and the parasites have mostly died off. You will keep them on the medicine for the last two weeks.

"There is *one thing*, though. Romeo seems to have an *aneurysm* on his aorta."

Kate gulps. "What does this mean?"

"It's a bulging on the blood vessel. Probably caused by the parasites as they sometimes are known to nest there. Just like Roxie's nested in her throat. They're all dying off now, so there's a chance it could heal completely over time, but sometimes the bulge will *not* go down."

"Yikes! What can be done about it?"

"There's really not much that can be done," he says. "There's a chance it could go away. But don't worry about it. Sometimes an aneurysm can be there for years and nothing ever happens." He looks at them soberly and says, "I must tell you, there *is* a chance it could burst. And in that case, it *could be fatal*."

He pauses and takes a deep breath as we all try to take in this information. "He may live a long and happy life. So, enjoy your lives. Take him on walks. Let him have a normal life. There's not really anything that anyone can do." Kate and Horace and Roxie and I all look at each other pondering his words. We aren't sure what it all means.

In the car going home, Roxie says to me, "You won't die! If anyone was going to die, I thought I came pretty close myself. And now look at me. I'm feeling more like my old self every day." Sometimes she knows just the right thing to say. *I love this dog!*

We ride back home in silence.

My eyes stay open the whole night, thinking. I sure don't want to die, but if I did die, I wonder if I would come back again as a different animal. I wondered about that ever since the day Kate talked about her past life experience. She said she lived with elephants in a different life. Maybe she even *was* an elephant. I hope she will talk about that again.

Maybe when you die, it's not too bad. Kate saw Marcello in her dream. He looked happy and *he told her not to worry*. I also consider the fact that I have gone through so much in life and learned more lessons than most dogs do. *Maybe that is the purpose of life?* To overcome adversities and become strong and happy? If that's true, then *I certainly have gone the distance.*

Death is such a puzzling topic. I could have easily died in the gutter as a young puppy or in the shelter when they ran out of space. And in Africa, we sure had a frightening brush with danger. I feel that I have already come close to death and come out on the other side. I like the idea that *life could go on*. But all the heavy thoughts finally weigh me down with a feeling that I will never know for sure. I don't remember if I decided not to worry about it, or I just succumbed to sleep.

***

The next morning, Kate reminds us we have two more weeks of medicine to go. She tells us, "After you have finished all your medications, we will go on a nice outing!" We get a little buzz and look at her with curiosity. She says we'll go to the Los Angeles Zoo.There's an event of the *Elephant Guardians*, who want to convince the zoo to free their elephant, Billy, and let him live at a sanctuary.

Kate says a sanctuary is a good place for elephants and other wildlife who were captured and put in zoos or circuses or anywhere else that was not natural to their native land and customs. Most captive wildlife has been removed from their families and habitats. So even if a zoo wants to let them retire, the animals would need some extra help and accommodations from humans, since they have lost their families. Sanctuaries create more natural settings where the animals are free to roam, and they receive help to make sure they are healthy and have good things to eat. Mom has visited a sanctuary in California called P.A.W.S.—Performing Animal Welfare Society. They have animals living there who took part in movies and television shows but are now living free and finding new friends. There's lots of space to explore, and they never have to do any work.

Roxie and I look at each other. We are always glad to learn something new about our fellow animals, especially elephants. We are ready to help! So next Saturday, we will be pleased to go to the Los Angeles Zoo to help Billy the elephant gain his freedom. The lazy days go by. We're both starting to feel pretty good and ready for some local adventures.

On Friday, Kate gives us our nice, warm baths, hair and teeth brushes, and hugs.

Next morning, I'm feeling sluggish, but I know I'll perk up when we get there. Kate is driving us across town to the zoo. We look out the window at all the traffic as we zip across the freeways of Los Angeles. Finally, we arrive at the zoo, park the car, and walk to the entranceway.

We see a good-sized crowd of protesters. Some activists are educating people who are leaving the zoo as well as talking to other people who were thinking of going in, but may change their minds. Some advocates are giving out pamphlets. Others are carrying big signs. Some of them have pictures of Billy in a small cage. We mill around with Mom. Lots of her friends are greeting her, and they're also greeting us.

A woman steps up to the microphone and welcomes everyone. Then we hear Kate get introduced at the podium: "We have a special guest today, Kate Amado, who has recently returned from Africa, where she lived with her father and her two dogs, Roxie and Romeo. She has been writing about wild African elephants for years, and she has been teaching young people about animals and conservation, both here and in Kenya." People clap.

Kate steps up with Roxie and me at her side, well behaved as always, chins high as we follow her proudly. She takes the microphone and says, "Billy the elephant has lived behind bars for decades. He is showing signs of stress, like other captive elephants. Head bobbing. Foot problems. A recent study shows that in captivity, large mammals suffer brain damage as well. He has suffered enough. It's time for the zoo to free Billy now!"

There are cheers in the crowd and a spontaneous chant. "Free Billy now! Free Billy now!"

Kate continues her talk. "We have recently returned from a two-year stay in Kenya where we saw and interacted with elephants in the wild. Elephant herds are nature's crowning glory. Their movements engender seed dispersal that results in forest growth. So we could positively say that *wild elephants directly affect the climate for all life on earth.*

"Elephants are kind: they help other animals in need. A wild elephant even helped our Roxie and Romeo escape from harm!" There are some *oohs* and *aahs* among the group. Kate looks down at us pups, and we both jump up a little and bark in unison. In a burst of enthusiasm, Kate reaches down and grabs the two of us and raises us to the microphone. "And Roxie and Romeo saved the elephant's life! And *that's* a juicy story for a novel!" There are a few chuckles in the crowd, followed by big applause. Everyone feels Kate's fervor. What they *can't* feel is our *canine* passion, which has also been ignited by our African experience.

When we go back to the sidelines, people come over and pet us and want to know all about us and our mom. Mommie smiles at us. We all feel exhilarated.

After we say our goodbyes, Kate lets us know she has some treats in her pockets and asks us, do we want to stop at a park on the way home? Yes, we do. So we head to Clover Park, our old haunt. We always loved its big trees, expansive fields, and walkways.

Chapter 25

ROXIE – Clover Park

Here we are, back at our neighborhood park. It has a familiarity about it and great smells. We take a leisurely stroll towards the back of the park. It's not too crowded today. Kate has called Horace and she says after our stroll, he'll meet us on the other side, and we can all go to lunch together.

Mom asks us if we want to run across the field. Romie and I give each other knowing looks and smiles. She unsnaps our leashes and we gambol through the tall green grasses in the field. We stretch and roll. The grass feels fresh, the air is clean. We see a lady with two small dogs way on the other side of the baseball field. We look up and Mom is smiling at them and heads in their direction. Mom and I pick up speed as we run downhill. When we get to the bottom, we are about to jog to the other side where the dogs are. Mom looks down at me.

I smile up at Mom. We look over at Romeo, only he's not there. Confused, we look all around and we don't see him. We look back up the little hill we ran down, and we see Romeo near the top.

He's not moving!

We race up the hill.

Romeo is on the ground. He's barely moving or breathing. We panic. Kate cries, "Help!" She calls Horace on her phone. "Dad, please hurry and come to the back of the park. There's something wrong with Romeo!"

We both sit down and cuddle his body. "Romie, come back! You are our special boy! We love you so much!" She cries. I lick his face.

**

Romeo thinks: I'm fading. If it's my time, I'm ready. What dog could have a better life than me? I love them. I love my life. I am a lucky dog. If there's another life, I will be sure to see them.

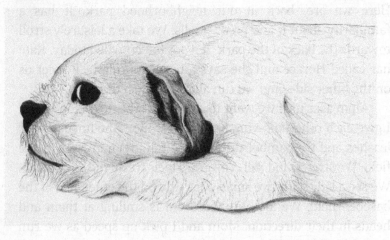

**

TWO WEEKS LATER

A section of the park in the back corner has been roped off around a couple of big trees. Our friends are standing around, acting solemn. There's Mom and Grandpa, and surprisingly

Grandma is also there. Ricarda is there. There are some of our friends and neighbors and Kate's friend Golda. Some of the people we saw at the L.A. Zoo are also there looking sad. Everyone, it seems, comes to hug Kate and me. Mommie and I have been crying all week. We haven't gotten much sleep. I've been sleeping next to her on the bed every night. She whispers to me and comforts me, and I kiss her and stay close.

There is a jar that has the remains of Romeo in it. Mom has gotten permission from the Parks Department to spread his ashes by these trees. She stands by the tree and everyone looks at her.

"Thank you for coming to pay honor to our Romeo. Roxie and I feel lost without him. As many of you know, he spent his early days in a gutter. His legs were damaged. Romeo was captured by a rescue worker in San Bernardino and he spent several weeks at the shelter. But due to his severe injuries, he was not comfortable, and there were limited accommodations for him. His days there were numbered. Fortunately, he was saved by wonderful volunteers from the Dexter Foundation and they saw that he received top treatment for his legs. He got a steel plate in his left leg and his recovery was long. As he was just finding his feet in foster homes, Roxie and I adopted him to be a lifelong companion for her and me.

"And what a funny, sweet companion he was. We all fell in love on the very day we met. Roxie and Romeo have been my best friends and inspiration in my work for animals. They came with me and my father, Horace, to Kenya to help save elephants—and help save they did. A famous elephant, Big Tusk, rescued Roxie and Romeo from elephant-poaching dognappers, and then Romeo rescued Big Tusk, who had been shot with a poison arrow. Even though it could have been a dangerous situation, Romeo refused to leave Big Tusk's side until he could get help. That was momentous. Roxie and Romeo were both awarded medals of honor by the officials of

Kenya for saving one of the last big tuskers."

She tears up and coughs. "What can we learn from Romeo's life?" She takes a long pause and seems to go inside her heart to get strength. Then, she speaks slowly, "What is the value of one little mutt?" She smiles and speaks clearly, "It is the sun and the moon and the stars."

I notice Grandma and Grandpa are crying and so is Ricarda and lots of people. Many come around Kate and hold her. She gathers her strength again and releases the ashes as she and I walk around the two big oak trees. People start singing a song called, "My Sweet Lord." I don't leave Kate's side.

Chapter 26

ROXIE AND KATE

THREE AND A HALF YEARS LATER

Kate and I are looking out the window of a small plane. It has started descending, and there's a great view of the palm trees, tropical plants, and the beautiful, glorious beach. My stomach isn't bothering me and excitement is filling my veins. "Look, Roxie! That's where you learned to swim! Remember?" I smile at her and she hugs me and kisses my head.

As the plane crawls to its position, we can see Hari and Roselyn, who are meeting us at the airport. Kate has tears in her eyes.

Roselyn squeals with delight. "Oh, Kate!" They give each other a big hug.

Hari reaches out his arms, surrounding all. Rosie picks me up. "Roxie! Sweet Roxie! I'm so glad to see you too!" Then to Kate, "It's so strange not having Romeo with you."

Kate says, "I know how much he would have loved to be here. He loved Kenya! Roxie misses him. We all miss him. I didn't think we would bring the dogs back to Africa, since traveling with them is so challenging. But they have loosened some of the restrictions, and I couldn't leave Roxie behind!"

I lick Roselyn's hand and also Hari's. Everyone is smiling.

"And how is Horace doing?"

Kate says, "Surprisingly, Grandpa got back together with Grandma! Ever since we had gone to visit her for Christmas a few years ago, she and Horace started talking on the phone and becoming more friendly. She had to undergo a minor medical procedure, and he became so concerned that he decided to go up to Oregon and hold her hand. And I guess they haven't stopped holding hands since. You know their divorce never was finalized, so they just got back to the old married couple they used to be. They felt their differences did not take away from their love and the good feelings they still had for each other! He sends his love to all."

Hari comes over to Kate. "I'm so happy we can see the completion of this mutual dream we shared. I couldn't have done it without you."

Kate blushes and says, "Well, I *know* I couldn't have done it without you, too. "

Hari says that his mother and cousins have prepared a banquet to celebrate our return to Kenya. "We're all hoping you and Roxie can come to my mother's farm for a big celebration while you are here."

Kate smiles broadly and says, "Yes, of course, we'd love to—and thank you!"

Roselyn says, "It's great that you could come. We'll finally celebrate the inauguration of the Elephant Matriarch School!"

Kate says, "We wouldn't miss it! And Hari has been working so hard getting it together. It'll be wonderful!"

Two nicely dressed younger women come running over to us with big smiles on their faces. "Kate!" Hugs all around. "We're so happy to see you. We wouldn't miss meeting you!"

Kate says, "Agnes and Mwaka! My best students! You both look wonderful! Now you are teachers in training! Are you both ready for the opening day?"

The young women laugh. Agnes says, "Yes! With our brand-new teaching certificates!"

"We'll work with a few more experienced teachers at the school," says Mwaka.

"Hi, Roxie!" the girls cheer.

I remember them. They both came to our award ceremony with the governor.

Kate says, "Before you know it, you two will be running the place."

Agnes says, "Why not? With the training we got from you, we're in good shape. I've also started working part-time with the Wildlife Service. Do you know a small herd of elephants has started coming back to the area?"

Kate says, "How wonderful! I've heard you guys have had a lot of flooding these past few years. That might help attract the elephants back."

"Maybe if we're lucky, we'll see them while you're here," Agnes says.

Kate says, "I really hope so. That would be the icing on the cake!"

We're both tired from our long journey and Hari drives us to our apartment. We're going to stay at the Wayside Apartments that we know so well. I'm excited. And I'm also feeling nostalgic. I think about the first time we came here with Romeo. I have a few moments of feeling very sad. Then I remember Amigo. I wonder if Amigo still lives there.

We get to the front gate. Renson and Jackie come running out to greet us. They are so happy to see us. Everyone has tears. Here comes Amigo. He is smiling and jumping for joy! He comes over to me. "Princess Warrior!" We rub noses and look in each other's eyes. I hope we get a chance to walk on the beach together again.

"Oh, Amigo!" says Kate, as he jumps up and towers over

her like old times.

Jackie says, "My boys and I sometimes take Amigo home with us at night so he won't be lonesome and get into trouble. Mostly I'm here, so if the boys don't have somewhere to take him, I bring him back to Wayside with me. He sure has missed you guys! He still loves to jump and swim in the ocean."

Suddenly, we hear loud monkey chattering. The trees are full of our old friends!

"Listen to that," Jackie says. They all came to say hello." We all laugh.

The next few days, we revisit Kokko's Coffee Shop and Nomads. Mom takes me for walks on the beach and some of the old beachboys remember us from before. We take a dip in the water. Romie and I were lucky to have this experience. I feel that his spirit is here with us.

One evening, Hari drives us over to his mother's farm for a huge celebration dinner. Everyone treats Kate like a queen and me like a princess. They let me play in the yard with their chickens, who are all so colorful and noisy. Mostly I just watch from nearby. But when they start to get used to me, they come and explore. I am mature enough not to chase them away and can just enjoy their company.

Hari makes a toast to Kate and me and even to Romeo. He says we have done so much to help his county and his country and that we are honored guests. Then he says to Kate, "We all are hoping that you will stay here with us. We need you and want you to have a happy life here." Everyone puts up their glasses and toasts us, and then they clap.

Kate seems overwhelmed and thanks them for their faith and trust in her. She says, "I know it's not always easy when we come from such different backgrounds. But when it comes to helping save those who need us most, like young moms and endangered animals, we can definitely put our heads together to create great solutions."

Hari comes over to Kate and says quietly, "I personally will be very happy if you stay and will do whatever I can to make your life happy."

Mom blushes and smiles at him. She chuckles and says, "Thank you. You've been great to work with. You offered me a good job and have always been on my side."

A rugged and stunning-looking man, very well-groomed, comes up behind Hari to shake Kate's hand. Hari introduces him. "This is John. He's the new supervisor and liaison of schools and wildlife in this area. He's promised to do all he can to help us succeed."

Kate smiles, extends her hand to John, and says, "Thank you so much for helping our plans come to life." John smiles broadly at her, all his teeth showing.

"The pleasure is all mine. I look forward to working with you in the future, and I thank you for all your brilliant ideas. I hope we can partner on many projects together." Then he pats my head and winks at me. Kate blushes, and there seems to be electricity in the air.

Later, Rosie tells her, "John's wife died a few years ago and he is alone, *like you are.*" They give each other girlie looks and they both crack up.

***

A few days later, we are getting ready for the opening day of the Elephant Matriarch School. Roselyn, Mwaka, and Agnes come to visit us at Wayside to talk about the official ceremonies. The governor and lots of spectators will be there to help celebrate the opening of the new school. Everyone is so excited.

Agnes says, "I think the elephant herd that has been returning to the Shimba Hills area has been seen near the school."

Kate responds, "What a great opening that would be if they came around, as they are the inspiration for the school. Agnes and Mwaka, remember when we were at AfricaGirls and there were monkeys running through the yard? I asked you girls what kind of monkeys they were, and nobody knew. That was one of the first days I was there."

"It's hard to remember," says Agnes. After all the work we did at Colobus Conservation, added on to your lessons and films, now we are experts!"

Everyone laughs.

Kate and I rest and take more long walks and swims at the beach while we wait for the school inauguration day. I play with Amigo.

***

The opening day finally arrives. Kate and I ride over to the school in Hari's car, and we leave extra early so we can see that everything is in order. Just after he parks the car, we spot a young elephant nearby on the hill. He is wandering around, nibbling on the grasses. Hari, Kate, and I get out and find a good spot to look at him.

He is standing outside the fence, very close. We walk in his direction. He spots us. Instead of running the other way, he comes straight toward us. In fact, he is looking at us. And he appears to be smiling. He comes over and stretches his trunk to sniff me and Mom.

There is something very familiar about this elephant. He puts his trunk right on Mom's face, as if he is giving her a kiss. She giggles and laughs. Then he puts his trunk on the top of my head and pets me with it. I give a short bark. He answers with a kind of chirping sound. I bark again. He makes his sound again. I keep barking and he continues to make sounds, little trumpeting sounds of a young elephant. Back and forth.

Soon we are singing together! Then he spins around! My heart is pounding a mile a minute. He spins the other way around!

Mom is astounded too. Mwaka and Agnes join us. They are both laughing. Rosie comes over to join the fun. Mom asks her, "Do you know anything about this elephant?"

Rosie, who used to work at the Shimba Hills National Reserve, says, "Yes. The little herd migrated here about two years ago. We had some floods that year, and a new river was created in the plains. No one knows exactly where it started. So everyone calls it the *Roaming River*. This young elephant was born on the riverbed, so he has been called *Roamie*—as the first elephant to be born after the rains and in our area."

Mommie tries to stifle herself from crying and laughing at the same time. She picks me up and gives me a hug. We go back to the place in the fence where Roamie is, and she pets him. She holds me up to him and we all look into each other's eyes. He startles us with another short trumpet. Then he spins around again and dances away from us in a funny way that makes us laugh.

That's when I look at Kate. We are both overcome. I give her a kiss. She laughs. And then I realize for sure—*we have all come back home!*

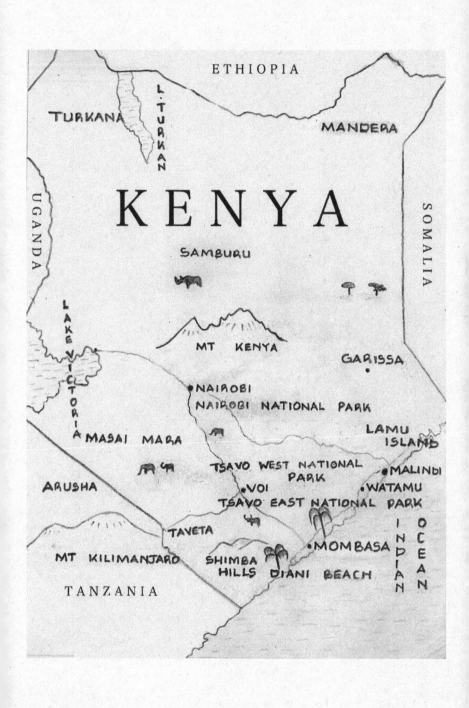

List of Illustrators

CHAPTER 1   s_draw - *Fiverr*

CHAPTER 2   pg. 29 - Moses Mugasia Misigo

                           pg. 31 - Moses Mugasia Misigo

CHAPTER 3   Moses Mugasio Migiso

CHAPTER 4   pg. 45 - Hilton Mghanga Mwakima

                           pg. 47 - Hilton Mghanga Mwakima

CHAPTER 5   pg. 51 - Hilton Mghanga Mwakima

                           pg. 58 - israelbuhian - *Fiverr*

CHAPTER 6   israelbuhian - *Fiverr*

CHAPTER 7   editing_zon3 - *Fiverr*

CHAPTER 8   pg. 78 - dipalutta - *Fiverr*

                           pg. 79 - Moses Mugasia Misigo

                           pg. 80 - Moses Mugasia Misigo

CHAPTER 9   s_draw - *Fiverr*

CHAPTER 10   pg. 94 - Hilton Mghanga Mwakima

                           pg. 97 - Hilton Mghanga Mwakima

CHAPTER 11   editing_zon3 - *Fiverr*

CHAPTER 12   dipalutta - Fiverr

CHAPTER 13   editing_zon3 - *Fiverr*

CHAPTER 14   s_draw - *Fiverr*

CHAPTER 15   editing_zon3 - *Fiverr*

CHAPTER 16   Moses Mugasia Misigo

CHAPTER 17   Moses Mugasia Misigo

CHAPTER 18   s_draw - *Fiverr*

CHAPTER 19   Hilton Mghanga Mwakima

CHAPTER 20   Hilton Mghanga Mwakima

CHAPTER 21   mauvinezohor205 - *Fiverr*

CHAPTER 22   akhter_a - *Fiverr*

CHAPTER 23   s_draw - *Fiverr*

CHAPTER 24   Gerald E. Jones

CHAPTER 25   Hilton Mghanga Mwakima

CHAPTER 26   Moses Mugasia Misigo

MAP   Hilton Mghanga Mwakima

KENYAN ARTISTS

Hilton Mghanga Mwakima may be reached at
mwakimahilton@yahoo.com

Moses Mugasia Misigo may be reached at
mogasiamoses1@gmail.com

GET INVOLVED!

So many wonderful organizations are helping animals and our world. Some of our favorites:

IN KENYA

Sheldrick Wildlife Trust: *sheldrickwildlifetrust.org*
The most successful orphan elephant rescue and rehabilitation in the world, including wildlife veterinary assistance, safe-guarding the natural environment and engendering community involvement

Elephant Voices: *www.elephantvoices.org*
Based on years of continuing research, has created the Elephant Ethnogram, a massive library of elephant behavior

Amboseli Trust: *www.elephanttrust.org*
Works to insure long-term conservation and welfare of African elephants through scientific research

Big Life Foundation: *biglife.org*
Partners with local communities and protects over 1.6 million acres of wilderness for all, employing hundreds of local Masai rangers and supporting education projects

Colobus Conservation: *colobusconservation.org*
Designed to promote the conservation, preservation and protection of primates like the threatened Angolan Colobus monkey and its coastal forest habitat in southeastern Kenya

Elephant Matriarch School Project: _georjaumano.com_
A program in the works to help young mothers in southern
Kenya become nature protectors and community leaders

IN THE U.S.A.

The Pet Show: _www.thepetshow.com_
Nationally syndicated radio show with pet therapist Warren
Eckstein. Thirty-one years on the air: the most trusted pet
expert in the U.S.

Nonhuman Rights Project: _nonhumanrightsproject.com_
The only civil rights organization in the US working to achieve
legal rights for members of species other than our own.

The Dexter Foundation: _www.dexterfoundation.com_
Dedicated to rescuing dogs in the Southern California area and
finding them forever homes

Society for the Prevention of Cruelty to Animals:
www.spcala.com
Independent animal welfare organization and shelter since
1877. They prevent cruelty to animals through education, law
enforcement, intervention, & advocacy.

WORLDWIDE

People for the Ethical Treatment of Animals: www.peta.org
PETA creates animal campaigns and investigations to help
animals around the world, endorse animal rights, support a
plant-based diet, and reach out to the younger generation to
endorse kindness.

Wildlife SOS: wildlifesos.org
Here is a comprehensive approach to saving India's wildlife through rescue and rehabilitation, including the first elephant hospitals and care centers, and reaching out to the abused and forgotten animals. They have rescued all the "dancing bears" and reach out to the poor communities who exploited wildlife and educate them in new skills.

Animal Defenders International: www.ad-international.org
ADI has a worldwide reputation for providing video and photographic evidence exposing the behind-the-scenes suffering in industry and supporting this evidence with scientific research. ADI rescues animals all over the world and educates the public on animals and environmental issues. They have returned imprisoned circus animals to their native lands in South America and maintain sanctuaries in South Africa, where they have transported 33 lions from the Americas.

Acknowledgements

Roxie and Romeo have inspired me from day one. I hope this story has captured their spirits and done justice to two extraordinary canines. Pictured with them on the cover is one of my adopted baby elephants at Sheldrick Wildlife Trust, Niglai.

Thank you to all the sweet elephants and adopted babies at Sheldrick Wildlife Trust whose charisma has continually brought me back to Kenya for more. And I am very grateful to my many wonderful friends around the world who also cherish elephants and take actions to protect them.

Thank you so much to Hilton Mghan Mwakima and Moses Mugasia Misigo, Kenyan artists who have delighted me with their work and whose illustrations are featured throughout *Terriers in the Jungle*.

I am most grateful to my husband, Gerald Everett Jones, for supporting me throughout this project and so many others.

I feel much gratitude to Golda David, my best writing teacher ever, and to her decades of supportive friendship which have meant the world to me.

I wish to thank the numerous friends who have helped me as beta readers for this manuscript over a period of two and a half years. These include Shawn Brogan, Andy Rodman, Ann Early, Madeline Bernstein, Eileen Wu, Roberta Edgar, Joyce Poole, Judy Carmen and Daryl Mori in the early versions, and

Robert J. Brunner, Marlaya Charleston, Barbara Hawkins, Katherine Kean, and Emilie Golding in later versions.

I especially thank Shawn Brogan and Rebecca Barker for believing in the project early on and nourishing me with their support from the beginning. I apologize to, and I am also thankful to anyone else who supported me and whom I may have inadvertently left out.

I am also grateful to the publisher and editors of Atmosphere Press for believing in me and the story, especially Nick Courtright, Kyle McCord, Ronaldo Alves, Erin Larson, and Cameron Finch.

About the Author

Georja Umano is a vegan animal activist who has organized, spoken and written about animals and animal causes in the US, Italy and Kenya, especially in the fields of elephant and wildlife conservation and canine companions.

Georja is a film, TV and theatre actress, stand-up comedian, and feature journalist. She's also worked as a credentialed adult education teacher and a children's nature docent.

She created, produced and co-hosted with her dog the YouTube series, "The Georja and Marcello Show."

She holds an MA degree in Educational Theatre from New York University, and a BA degree in English Literature from LeMoyne College. For more information, please go to *http://GeorjaUmano.com*.

Terriers in the Jungle is her first novel.

CPSIA information can be obtained
at www.ICGtesting.com
Printed in the USA
LVHW090933310822
727260LV00005B/857